PERRAULT'S

Fairy Tales

ILLUSTRATED BY
JANUSZ GRABIANSKI

TRANSLATED BY
ANNE CARTER

JONATHAN CAPE
THIRTY BEDFORD SQUARE
LONDON

This edition first published in Great Britain 1967
Reprinted 1969
Translation © 1967 by Jonathan Cape Ltd
Illustrations © 1967 by Verlag Carl Ueberreuter, Wien-Heidelberg

Jonathan Cape Ltd, 30 Bedford Square, London, WC1

SBN 224 61233 6

Contents

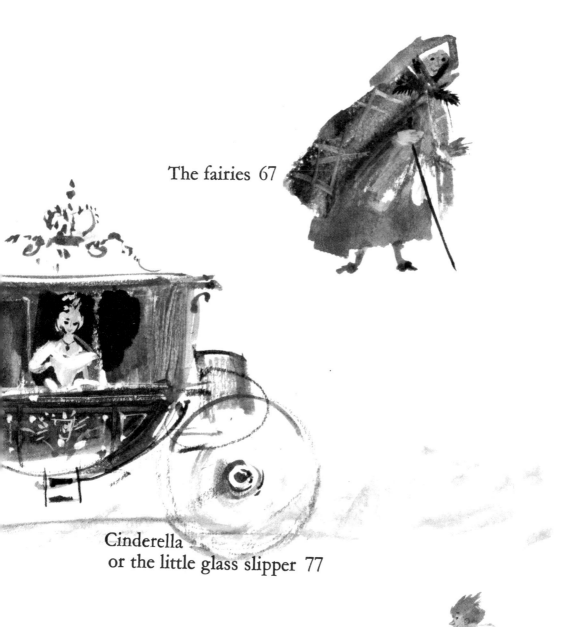

The sleeping beauty

Once upon a time there lived a king and a queen who had one great sorrow and it grieved them more than words can tell. They had no children. They travelled all over the world taking the waters, they made vows and pilgrimages, but all to no avail. Then, at long last, the queen found she was going to have a baby and in due course gave birth to a daughter.

There was a splendid christening and all the fairies to be found in that country (there were seven of them) were invited to be godmothers to the little princess, so that each might bring her a gift. This was the fairy custom in those days; the princess would thus be bound to possess every imaginable perfection.

After the christening service, all the guests went back to the king's palace where a great banquet was held in honour of the fairies. Everything was set out with the utmost magnificence and before each fairy's place was a solid golden casket containing a knife, fork and spoon of pure gold inlaid with diamonds and rubies. But just as they were all sitting down an aged fairy stalked into the room. She had not been invited because for more than fifty years she had not set foot outside the tower that was her home, and everyone thought she was either dead or under a spell.

The king had a place set for her at the table, but he could not give her solid gold plate like the others because only seven sets had been made for the seven fairies. The old fairy thought she had been deliberately insulted and mumbled threats under her breath.

Hearing this, one of the young fairies who was sitting next to her guessed that the hag might give the little princess some

dreadful gift. When they all left the table she hid behind a tapestry so that she would be the last to speak and might be able to some extent to undo any harm the old fairy should bring about.

Presently the fairies began to give their gifts to the princess. The youngest promised that she should be the loveliest girl in the world, the next that she should be angelically good and clever, the third that she should bring an enchanting grace to everything she did, the fourth that she should dance to perfection, the fifth that she should sing like a nightingale and the sixth that she should possess a magic touch on every musical instrument.

Now it was the old fairy's turn. Her head was quivering more from spite than from age as she foretold that the princess would prick her finger on a spindle and die. At this dreadful gift a shudder ran through the entire court, and there were tears in every eye.

At that moment the young fairy stepped out from behind the tapestry.

'Be comforted, Your Majesties,' she said clearly. 'Your daughter shall not die. It is true that I have not the power to undo all that my elder has done. The princess will cut her finger on a spindle but, instead of dying, she will only fall into a deep sleep for a hundred years. At the end of that time a king's son shall come and wake her.'

In an attempt to prevent the disaster foretold by the hag, the king straightway issued an edict forbidding anyone to use a spinning wheel or have a spindle in the house, on pain of death.

Fifteen or sixteen years went by, until the king and queen

happened to be staying at one of their castles in the country. The young princess was exploring the castle one day. She went from room to room and at last climbed to the very top of one of the towers. There, in a tiny garret, she found a little old woman, sitting all alone and spinning. The poor old soul had never heard of the king's order forbidding the use of spinning wheels.

'Good woman, what are you doing?' asked the princess.

'I am spinning, my dear,' replied the old woman, not knowing who she was.

'Oh,' said the princess, 'how lovely. How do you do it? Give it to me and let me see if I can do as well.'

No sooner had she taken it than, partly because she was in too much of a hurry and a little awkward, but also because it had been ordained by fairy command, she pricked her finger and fell down senseless.

The old woman was terribly upset and screamed for help. People came running from all directions. They splashed water on the princess's face, they loosened her dress, rubbed her hands and bathed her forehead with eau de cologne, but nothing would revive her. Then the king, who had been brought upstairs by the noise, remembered the fairy prophecy and knew that what the fairies had said was bound to come true. He had the princess laid on a bed embroidered all over with gold and silver in the finest apartment in the palace.

She was so beautiful that she looked like an angel lying there. Even in a trance her complexion was as fair as ever, her cheeks were rosy and her lips like coral. Only her eyes were closed,

but her soft breathing could still be heard to show that she was not dead. The king gave orders that she should be left to sleep in peace until the time came for her to wake.

When the accident to the princess happened, the good fairy who had saved her life by ordaining that she should sleep for a hundred years was twelve thousand miles away in the kingdom of Mataquin. But she heard about it at once from a little dwarf who had a pair of seven-league boots. (These were boots that carried their wearer seven leagues in a single stride.) The fairy set out at once and an hour later she was seen arriving in a fiery chariot drawn by dragons.

The king stepped forward to hand her out of her chariot. The fairy thoroughly approved of everything he had done but, being a far-sighted fairy, she thought that when the princess came to wake up she would be very frightened, all alone in the old castle. So this is what she did.

She waved her wand over everyone in the castle (except the

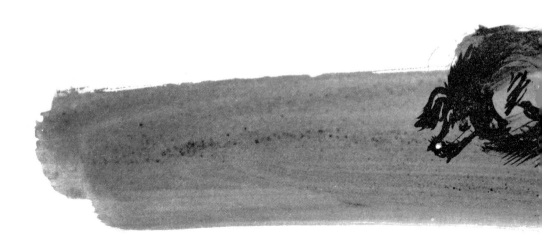

king and queen): governesses, ladies-in-waiting, chambermaids, gentlemen, officers, stewards, cooks, scullions, errand boys, guards, porters, pages and footmen. She touched all the horses in the stables as well, with their grooms, the big mastiffs in the courtyard and even the princess's own little dog, Puff, who was lying beside her on the bed. As she touched them, they all fell asleep to waken only at the same time as their mistress, and be there still ready to serve her when she needed them. Even the spits by the fire with their load of pheasants and partridges, even the fire itself slept. All this happened in an instant, for fairies work very fast.

Then the king and queen kissed their dear, sleeping daughter and went away from the castle. They proclaimed throughout the land that no one was to go near it. But there was no need for the decree, because within a quarter of an hour a deep forest had grown up round the park, with trees of all sizes and such a tangle of thorns and brambles that neither man nor beast could force a way through. All that could be seen of the castle was the distant tops of its towers. None doubted that this too was the work of the fairy, so that the princess should be safe from prying eyes while she slept.

At the end of a hundred years, when the crown had passed to a different family from that of the sleeping princess, the son of the reigning king happened to be hunting in the same part of the country. He saw the towers rising above the huge, dense wood and asked what they were. Each one told him the story as he had heard it: some said it was an old, haunted castle, others that

all the witches in the land held their sabbaths there. The most general belief was that it was the home of an ogre who carried off to it all the children he caught and devoured them at his leisure without fear of pursuit, since he was the only person who could pass through the wood.

The prince was wondering what to make of it, when an old peasant took up the story.

'Your Highness,' he said, 'more than fifty years ago I heard my father say that there was a princess in the castle, the loveliest lady ever seen. She was destined to sleep for a hundred years and would be wakened by the king's son for whom she waits.'

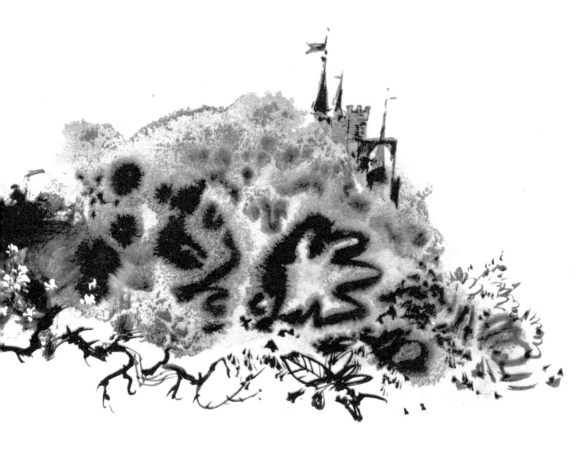

Fired by the tale, the young prince knew at once that it was for him to bring this noble adventure to its end. Spurred on by love and honour, he resolved to discover the truth forthwith.

Scarcely had he moved a step towards the forest when all the great trees, all the thorns and brambles parted instantly to let him through. He saw the castle at the end of a long ride and walked towards it. As he went inside he was a little surprised to see that none of his retinue had been able to follow him because the trees had closed in again as soon as he passed through. However, a prince who is young and in love is always brave, and so he went on undeterred into the huge forecourt. At first sight, what he found there was enough to freeze him with terror. There was a dreadful silence and the presence of death seemed all around, with the figures of men and animals lying as if dead. But the pimply noses and rosy faces of the porters soon showed him that they were only asleep, while the dregs of wine in their glasses made it clear they had nodded off in the very act of drinking.

The prince went on into a great, marble-paved courtyard and climbed the stairs to the guard-room where the soldiers lined the walls, their muskets on their shoulders, and all snoring

lustily. He passed through a number of rooms crowded with lords and ladies, some sitting down and others standing, but all fast asleep.

At last he came to a room all decorated in gold, and there was the loveliest thing he had seen in all his life. There, on a bed with the curtains drawn back on every side, lay a princess, apparently about fifteen or sixteen years old, whose beauty glowed with a fairy radiance.

Trembling with awe, he drew nearer and knelt down beside her. As he did so the spell was broken, and the princess awoke, and smiled at him as tenderly as if she had known him all her life.

'Is it you, my prince?' she said. 'I have waited so long for you.'

These words, and still more the way in which they were spoken, so charmed the prince that he could scarcely express his joy and thankfulness and could only protest that he loved her more than anything on earth. But though he stammered, his words pleased all the more, containing little eloquence, but a great deal of love. She was less tongue-tied than he, which is not to be wondered at since she had had a long time to dream about what she would say to him. It seems (although the story says nothing about it) that the good fairy had sent her pleasant dreams to while away her long sleep. They talked for four hours and still had not said half the things they wanted to say to one another. But the whole palace had woken with the princess, and everyone set about their business. Moreover, since they were not all of them

in love, they were soon dying of hunger. At last, the princess's lady-in-waiting, who was as hungry as anyone, lost patience and said right out that dinner was on the table.

The prince helped the princess to rise. She was fully dressed in the most magnificent clothes and the prince was careful not to tell her that her dress, with its great starched ruff, would have been fashionable in his grandmother's day. And in fact she was none the less lovely for that.

They dined in a great mirrored hall, waited on by all the princess's household. Viols and hautboys played ancient tunes that were still sweet though they had not been played for close on a hundred years. Afterwards, as soon as they had finished dinner, the royal chaplain married them in the castle chapel, the lady-in-waiting drew the curtains on them and they were left alone.

They did not sleep very much, indeed the princess hardly needed to, and first thing in the morning the prince left her to make his way back to the city, where he knew his father would be worried about him.

The prince told his father he had been lost out hunting in the forest but had spent the night in a charcoal-burner's hut and eaten his black bread and cheese. His father the king was a simple man and believed him, but his mother had her doubts. When she saw that he went hunting nearly every day and always had a good excuse to offer when he spent two or three nights away from home, she felt quite certain that he had a sweetheart somewhere.

The prince and princess lived together like this for two whole years and they had two children. The first was a girl and was named Dawn, and the second, a boy, was called Day because he looked even more beautiful than his sister.

The prince never dared tell the queen his secret. Although he loved her, he was afraid of her too, because she came of a family of ogres and the king had only married her for her great wealth.

It was even whispered secretly at court that she had some ogrish tendencies and whenever she saw little children going by had

25

great difficulty in preventing herself from pouncing on them. Naturally, the prince did not feel like telling her anything.

But at the end of two years the king died and the prince became the ruler. Then he proclaimed his marriage to everyone and went in state to fetch his queen from her castle.

She made a splendid entry into the capital city, with her two children beside her.

Some time later, the king went to war with his neighbour, the Emperor Cantalabutte. He left the queen mother as regent of the kingdom and entrusted his wife and children to her care.

The king was to be away at the war for the whole summer. He was no sooner gone than the queen mother sent her daughter-in-law and the two children to a country house deep in the forest, where she would be able to satisfy her horrid desires more easily. She herself followed a few days later and one evening she told her majordomo:

'I will eat baby Dawn for my dinner tomorrow.'

'Oh, Madam!' gasped the majordomo.

'That is my order,' said the queen, in the voice of an ogress craving human flesh. 'I will have her served with a *sauce Robert*,' she added.

The poor man saw that it was no use defying an ogress, so he took his big knife and went upstairs to little Dawn's room. At that time she was four years old and she came bouncing up to him, laughing and flinging her arms round his neck to ask for sweets. The knife fell from his hand, and he burst into tears and went out into the yard to kill a lamb instead. He made such an

appetizing sauce to go with it that his mistress told him she had
never eaten anything so delicious.

As for little Dawn, he had taken her away and given her to his
wife to hide in their house at the far end of the kitchen yard.

A week later, the wicked queen told her majordomo:

'I will eat baby Day for my supper.'

The majordomo said nothing, but made up his mind to trick
her as he had done before. He went to look for little Day and
found him with a toy foil in his hand, playing at fencing with a
pet monkey, although he was only three years old. He carried him
down to his wife who hid him with little Dawn. Instead of baby
Day, the majordomo served up a tender young kid which the
ogress ate with huge relish.

So far, so good. But one evening the wicked queen said to her majordomo:

'I will eat the queen with the same sauce as her children.'

This time the poor majordomo despaired of being able to outwit her. The young queen was over twenty, not counting the hundred years she had been asleep, and although her skin was white and lovely, she was bound to be a little tough. How could he find an animal that would have the right degree of toughness? To save his own life, he resolved to kill the queen and went up to her room, determined to do the thing once and for all. Working himself into a frenzy, he burst into the young queen's apartment, knife in hand, but he could not bear to take her unawares and explained with all due respect that he had been commanded to do it by the queen mother.

'Kill me!' she said, offering her neck. 'Carry out your orders. I shall go to join my children, my poor children whom I loved so dearly!'

The children had been taken away without a word to her and she believed they were dead.

The poor majordomo relented. 'No, no, my lady,' he told her, 'you shall not die, although you shall join your children. But it will be in my house, where I have hidden them. I am going to trick the queen again and give her a young doe to eat in your place.'

He took her straight to his quarters and left her there, hugging and crying over her children, while he went to prepare a doe for the ogress's supper. The ogress ate it as greedily as if it had really been the young queen, feeling highly delighted with her cruelty and quite prepared to tell the king when he came home that his queen and her children had all been devoured by savage wolves.

One evening, however, as she was prowling round the kitchen quarters of the castle, sniffing after fresh meat, as she often did, she happened to hear little Day crying because his mother was going to spank him for being naughty. And she heard little Dawn as well, begging for her brother to be forgiven.

When the ogress recognized the voices of the queen and her children and knew she had been tricked, she flew into a fearful

rage. The next morning, in a voice so terrible that everyone quailed at the sound, she ordered a huge vat to be carried into the middle of the courtyard and filled with adders, toads and all kinds of venomous snakes. The queen and her children, the major-domo, his wife and their maid were all to be thrown into it. She had given orders for them to be brought out with their hands tied behind their backs.

Just as they were standing there, with the executioners ready to hurl them into the vat, who should ride into the courtyard but the king! No one had expected him so soon, but he had galloped post haste and was now gazing in astonishment and demanding an explanation of the ghastly scene. No one dared enlighten him, but then the ogress, mad with fury at what she saw, suddenly plunged head first into the vat, where the evil creatures she had put there quickly made an end of her. The king was naturally upset, because after all she was his mother, but he was soon comforted by having his lovely wife and children safe.

Little Red Riding Hood

Once upon a time there was a little country girl, the prettiest ever seen. Her mother doted on her and her grandmother adored her. The old woman made her a little scarlet hood which suited her so well everyone called her Little Red Riding Hood.

One day, when Little Red Riding Hood's mother had baked some cakes, she said to her:

'Go and see how your grandmother is, because I heard she was not very well. Take her a cake and this little pot of butter.'

Little Red Riding Hood set off at once for her grandmother's cottage which was in another village. She was going through a wood when she met old man Wolf. He would have liked to eat her up, but he did not dare to because there were several woodcutters about in the forest. Instead, he asked her where she was going. Not knowing that it was dangerous to stop and listen to a wolf, the poor child told him:

'I am going to see my grandmother, to take her a cake and a little pot of butter from my mother.'

'Does she live far away?' asked the wolf.

'Oh, yes,' Little Red Riding Hood told him, 'it is away beyond the mill you can see, right over there, the first house in the village.'

'Well now,' said the wolf, 'I should like to go and see her too. I shall take this path and you that one, and we'll see who gets there first.'

The wolf began to run as hard as he could along the shortest path, and the little girl went on by the longer way, amusing herself by picking nuts, chasing butterflies and gathering bunches of wild flowers as she went.

Very soon the wolf came to the grandmother's cottage and knocked on the door: rat tat.

'Who's there?'

'It's your granddaughter, Little Red Riding Hood,' said the wolf, disguising his voice. 'I've brought you a cake and a little pot of butter from my mother.'

The good grandmother was in bed because she was not feeling very well, and she called out: 'Pull out the pin and the latch will come up.'

The wolf pulled out the pin and the door opened. He sprang on the old woman and ate her up in less than no time, because he had eaten nothing for three days.

Then he shut the door and lay down in the grandmother's bed to wait for Little Red Riding Hood. It was not long before she came and knocked on the door: rat tat.

'Who's there?'

At first, when she heard the wolf's great big voice, Little Red Riding Hood was frightened, but then she decided her grandmother must have a cold and answered:

36

'It's your granddaughter, Little Red Riding Hood. I've brought you a cake and a little pot of butter from my mother.'

The wolf made his voice a little bit softer and called out: 'Pull out the pin and the latch will come up.'

Little Red Riding Hood pulled out the pin and the door opened. When the wolf saw her come in he got right down in the bed and hid under the covers and said: 'Put the cake and the little pot of butter on the shelf and come into bed with me.'

Little Red Riding Hood undressed and climbed into bed where she was very much surprised to see how her grandmother looked in her nightdress.

'Grandmother,' she said, 'what big arms you have!'

'All the better to hug you with, my dear.'

'Grandmother, what big legs you have!'

'All the better to run with, my dear.'

'Grandmother, what big ears you have!'

'All the better to hear with, my dear.'

'Grandmother, what big eyes you have!'

'All the better to see with, my dear.'

'Grandmother, what big teeth you have!'

'All the better to eat you with.'

And with these words the wicked wolf sprang on Little Red Riding Hood and gobbled her up.

Bluebeard

Once upon a time there was a man who had fine houses in town and country, gold and silver plate, richly embroidered furnishings and gilded carriages. But unfortunately for him, this man had a blue beard which made him so ugly and frightful that there was not a woman or girl who did not run away at the sight of him.

A neighbour of his, a lady of quality, had two ravishingly beautiful daughters. He asked for the hand of one of them in marriage, leaving it to her to choose which one she would bestow on him. Both girls were unwilling and tossed the proposal back and forth between them, neither being able to bring herself to accept a man with a blue beard. What put them off still further was the fact that he had already been married several times and no one knew what had become of his wives.

In order to improve their acquaintance, Bluebeard invited the girls with their mother and three or four of their best friends, as well as some young men of the neighbourhood, to spend a week at one of his country houses. They spent the time in a round of outings, hunting and fishing expeditions, dances, parties and picnics. They hardly ever went to bed at all, but stayed up all night playing jokes on one another.

In the end things went so well that the younger sister began to think that perhaps their host's beard was not so very blue after all, and that he was really a very nice man. The wedding took place as soon as they returned to town.

When a month had gone by, Bluebeard told his wife that he was obliged to go away on important business to a distant part of

the country, and would be gone for at least six weeks. He hoped she would enjoy herself while he was away and suggested that she might like to invite some of her friends and take them to the country. He wanted her to have a good time.

'Here', he told her,' are the keys of the two big store rooms. This one is for the gold and silver plate we do not use every day, and these are for my strong room, where I keep all my gold and silver, and for my coffers full of precious stones. This is the master key to all the rooms. As for this little key, it belongs to the small room at the end of the long gallery downstairs. Open everything, go everywhere, except for this one small room. That I forbid you to enter, and I forbid it so strictly that if you should open it you may expect no mercy from my anger.'

She promised to do exactly as he told her and he kissed her and climbed into his coach and was off.

Her friends and neighbours did not wait to be asked before calling on the young bride. They were bursting with impatience to see her magnificent house, but they had not dared to come while her husband was at home because they were frightened by his blue beard. There they all were on the instant swarming through the rooms and closets and boudoirs, each one finer than the last. Next they went up to the store rooms where the number of beautiful tapestries, beds, sofas, cabinets, pedestals and tables quite took their breath away. There were mirrors in which they could see themselves from top to toe, some with bevelled glass

43

frames, others of silver and silver gilt, and all the most beautiful and splendid ever seen. But although they never tired of envying their friend and marvelling at her good fortune, the girl herself found no pleasure in the sight of all these riches, because she was too eager to see inside the little room downstairs.

She was so overcome with curiosity that, without reflecting that it was hardly polite to leave her guests, she plunged down a back stairway at such a pace that two or three times she thought she would break her neck.

On reaching the door of the little room she paused for a moment remembering how her husband had warned her and wondering what terrible punishment would fall on her for disobeying. But the temptation was too strong for her to resist, and at last she took the little key and tremblingly opened the door of the room.

At first she could see nothing at all because the shutters were closed, but in a few moments she began to make out that the floor was quite covered with congealed blood and that mirrored in it were the dead bodies of a number of women hanging from the walls. These were all Bluebeard's former wives whom he had stabbed to death, one after the other.

Half dead with terror, she let the key of the room fall from her hand as she drew it out of the lock.

When she had recovered herself a little she picked up the key, locked the door again and went up to her own room to get over the shock. But she could not do so, she had been too shaken. Seeing that there were bloodstains on the key of the little room she wiped it two or three times, but the blood would not go away. No matter how much she washed it or rubbed it with sand and grit the blood was still there, for it was a magic key and there was no way of getting it quite clean. When the blood was wiped off one side it came back on the other.

That very same evening, Bluebeard returned from his journey. He said that he had received some letters on the way telling him

that the matter about which he was going had been settled to
his advantage. His wife did her best to look as though she was
delighted to have him back so quickly.

The next morning he asked for his keys, and her hand trembled
so much as she gave them to him that he easily guessed all that
had happened.

'How is it,' he said, 'that the key of the little room is not with
the rest?'

'I must have left it upstairs on my table,' she said.

'Be sure you give it to me soon,' said Bluebeard.

She put it off several times but at last she had to bring the
key. Bluebeard looked at it carefully and then said to his wife:
'Why is there blood on this key?'

'I don't know,' answered the poor woman, paler than death.

'You don't know?' echoed Bluebeard. 'I know very well.
You wanted to go inside the little room. Very well, my lady,
go inside it you shall, and take your place beside the ladies you
saw there.'

She threw herself at her husband's feet, weeping and begging
him, with every sign of real repentance, to forgive her for having
disobeyed him. She was lovely enough in her distress to have
melted a stone, but Bluebeard's heart was harder than any stone.

'You must die, lady,' he said, 'and at once.'

'If I must die,' she answered, gazing at him with eyes bathed
in tears, 'give me a little time to say my prayers.'

'I will give you just ten minutes,' Bluebeard told her, 'but
not one moment longer.'

The moment she was alone, the girl called her sister and said to her:

'Sister Anne (for this was her name), I implore you, climb up to the top of the tower and see if my brothers are coming. They promised to come and visit me today. And if you see them, signal to them to hurry.'

Her sister Anne climbed up to the top of the tower and every other second the wretched girl called out to her: 'Anne, sister Anne, can you see nothing coming?'

And her sister Anne replied: 'I see only the motes of dust in the sunshine and the bright green grass.'

Meanwhile Bluebeard, grasping a huge cutlass in his hand, was roaring with all his might: 'Come down quickly, or I will come up.'

'Please, just one more second,' answered his wife. Then she called up softly: 'Anne, sister Anne, can you see nothing coming?'

And her sister Anne replied: 'I can see nothing but the motes of dust in the sun and the bright green grass.'

'Come down now, quickly,' bellowed Bluebeard, 'or I will come up.'

'I am coming,' his wife answered, and then she called: 'Anne, sister Anne, can you see nothing coming?'

Sister Anne replied: 'I can see a great cloud of dust coming this way.'

'Is it my brothers?'

'Alas no, sister, I can see it is only a flock of sheep.'

'Will you come down?' roared Bluebeard.

'Just one moment more,' answered his wife. Then she called: 'Anne, sister Anne, can you see nothing coming?'

Her sister replied: 'I can see two horsemen coming this way but they are still a very long way off.'

'Thank Heaven,' she cried a moment later, 'it is our brothers. I am signalling to them as hard as I can to hurry.'

Bluebeard was now thundering so loudly that the whole house shook. The poor woman went down and flung herself at his feet, her hair falling about her tear-stained face.

'That will not help you,' said Bluebeard. 'You must die.'

Seizing her hair with one hand, he raised his cutlass with the other, and was on the point of slicing off her head. The poor woman turned a dying glance on him and begged for one more instant to prepare herself.

'No, no!' he said, 'commend yourself to heaven,' and he raised his arm –

At that moment there was such a hammering on the door that Bluebeard stopped short. The door burst open and in came two riders who drew their swords and rushed straight at him.

Seeing that they were his wife's brothers, one a dragoon, the other a musketeer, Bluebeard turned at once to flee. But the two brothers were so close on his heels that they caught him before he reached the steps. They plunged their swords into his body

and left him dead. The poor woman was almost as dead as her husband, and had not even the strength to fall into her brothers' arms.

It turned out that Bluebeard had no heirs and his wife remained mistress of all his wealth. She used some of it to enable her sister Anne to marry a young gentleman who had loved her for a long time, and some she spent to buy commissions for her two brothers.

She kept the rest for herself and married a good, kind man who made her forget the terrible time she had spent with Bluebeard.

Puss in boots

A certain miller had nothing to leave to his three sons but his mill, his donkey and his cat. These were quickly divided up without the help of lawyers or attorneys, who would soon have swallowed up the whole of the poor legacy.

The eldest had the mill. The second had the donkey. And the youngest had only the cat. He was bitterly disappointed at getting such a pathetic share.

'My brothers,' he said, 'will be able to earn a decent living by joining forces, but as for me, once I have eaten my cat and had his fur made into a muff, I shall just have to starve to death.'

The cat overheard this, although pretending not to be listening, and observed placidly: 'Don't worry, Master. All you have to do is to give me a bag and get me a pair of boots made for pushing through the undergrowth, and you will find that you have not got such a bad bargain as you think.'

The cat's master did not build any great hopes on this, but he had seen the animal perform a good many cunning tricks to catch rats and mice, such as hanging by his claws or hiding in the flour bin and shamming dead, and so he did not despair of finding some help in his plight.

When the cat was given the things he asked for, he pulled on his boots, slung the bag over his shoulder, holding on to the strings with his front paws, and set off in the direction of a warren where a great many rabbits were to be found. Putting a little bran and some lettuce in the bag, he then lay down as though he were dead and waited for some young rabbit who was not

yet up to all the tricks of the world to come along and burrow in the bag for the food he had put inside.

No sooner had he laid himself down than he was delighted to see a silly young rabbit walk straight into the bag. Puss promptly tightened the strings and caught and killed him without a moment's thought.

Feeling very pleased with his catch, he went at once to the royal palace and asked to speak to the king. He was shown up to His Majesty's apartments and, once there, he made the king a deep bow, saying:

'Here is a wild rabbit, Sire, which I have been sent to bring you on behalf of the marquis of Carabas.' (This was the name he had decided to call his master.)

'Tell your master,' the king replied, 'that we thank him for his gift which gives us great pleasure.'

Another time the cat went and hid himself in a cornfield, leaving the neck of his bag wide open. When a brace of partridges were safely inside, he pulled the strings tight and captured them both. Then he went to present them to the king, just as he had done with the wild rabbit. The king accepted the partridges with equal pleasure and gave the cat a little something for himself.

For two or three months the cat went on in this way, taking the king occasional presents of game from his master's coverts. Then one day he learned that the king was to take a drive along the river-bank, with his daughter, who was the most beautiful princess in the whole world.

'Now,' he said to his master, 'if you will follow my advice, your fortune is made. All you have to do is go for a swim in the river at the spot I shall show you, and leave the rest to me.'

The marquis of Carabas had no idea what good it would do him, but he did as his cat told him.

While he was swimming, the king came by and the cat began to shriek at the top of his voice:

'Help! Help! The marquis of Carabas is drowning!'

At these cries, the king put his head out of the carriage window and, recognizing the cat who had so often brought him game, he ordered his guards to hurry quickly to the rescue of the marquis of Carabas.

While they were pulling the poor marquis out of the river, the cat went up to the carriage and told the king that as his master

was bathing some thieves had come along and carried off all his clothes, although he had cried out 'Stop thief!' with all his might. The truth was that the rascal had hidden them under a stone.

The king immediately commanded the gentlemen of his wardrobe to go and fetch one of his own best suits for the marquis of Carabas.

The king treated the marquis with all possible kindness, and as the fine clothes he had been given set him off to great advantage (for he was a very handsome young man), the king's daughter was extremely taken with him. No sooner had the marquis of Carabas given her one or two fond, though perfectly respectful, glances than she was madly in love with him.

The king invited him to get into the carriage and continue the drive with them.

The cat, delighted to see his plan going so well, went on ahead and presently came upon some peasants hay-making.

'Look here, my good hay-makers,' he told them, 'unless you tell the king that the field you are mowing belongs to the marquis of Carabas, you will all be chopped into mincemeat.'

Sure enough, the king asked the hay-makers whose field they were mowing.

'It belongs to the marquis of Carabas,' they all answered together, terrified by the cat's threat.

'You have a fine estate,' said the king to the marquis of Carabas.

'As you see, Sire,' answered the marquis, 'this field yields a rich harvest every year without fail.'

The cat was still going on ahead and presently he came upon some harvesters.

'Look here, my good harvesters,' he told them, 'unless you say that all these cornfields belong to the marquis of Carabas, you will be chopped into mincemeat.'

A moment later the king passed by and inquired who owned all the cornfields he could see.

'The marquis of Carabas,' answered the harvesters.

The king congratulated the marquis.

All the way, the cat went ahead of the carriage and always said the same thing to everyone he met. The king was astounded at the great wealth of the marquis of Carabas.

At last the cat came to a splendid castle. It belonged to an ogre who was the richest ever seen, because all the lands the king had passed were part of his estates.

The cat had gone to some trouble to find out all about this ogre and his magic powers. Now he asked to speak to him, explaining that he had not liked to pass so close by his castle without having the honour of paying his respects.

The ogre welcomed him as politely as an ogre can and asked him to sit down.

'I have been told,' said the cat, 'that you have the power to change yourself into all kinds of animals: that you can turn yourself into a lion or an elephant, for instance.'

'It's quite true,' the ogre said gruffly, 'and just to show you, you shall see me become a lion.'

The cat was so frightened to find himself confronted with a lion that he promptly shot up into the rafters – not without a good deal of difficulty and danger on account of his boots, which were no good for walking on tiles. Some time later, when he saw that the ogre

62

had returned to his normal shape, he came down and admitted that he had been thoroughly scared.

'I have also been told,' he went on, 'although I can scarcely believe it, that you have the power to take the shape of the smallest animals as well – for instance, to change yourself into a rat or mouse. I must admit that I think this quite impossible.'

'Impossible!' roared the ogre. 'You shall see.'

Instantly he changed himself into a mouse and began to run about the floor. The cat no sooner saw this than he pounced on the mouse and ate it up.

63

Meanwhile the king came by and, seeing the ogre's splendid castle, was anxious to go inside.

The cat heard the noise of the carriage crossing the castle drawbridge and ran out to meet the king.

'Welcome, Your Majesty,' he cried, 'to the castle of the marquis of Carabas.'

'What, marquis?' exclaimed the king. 'Does this castle too belong to you? Nothing could be finer than this courtyard and the buildings round it. We should like to see inside, if you please.'

The king led the way. The marquis offered his arm to the young princess and they followed him up the steps into a great hall. There they found a magnificent banquet laid. The ogre had prepared it for some friends who were coming to visit him that very day, but when they found out that the king was there the other ogres had not dared to go in.

The king was as delighted with the excellent qualities of the marquis of Carabas as his daughter was, and she was head over heels in love with him. Seeing his great wealth and mellowed by five or six cups of wine, the king turned to his host and said:

'It is for you to say, my dear marquis, whether you will become my son-in-law.'

The marquis bowed deeply and accepted the honour done him by the king, and that very same day he and the princess were married.

As for the cat, he became a very great lord indeed and gave up chasing mice. Except, of course, for his own amusement.

The fairies

Once upon a time there was a widow who had two daughters. The elder was so like herself in looks and character that she might have been mistaken for her mother. They were both so proud and disagreeable that there was no living with them. But the younger daughter was just like her father, gentle and good, and the prettiest girl imaginable into the bargain.

Like being naturally drawn to like, the mother adored her elder daughter and heartily disliked the younger. She made her eat her meals in the kitchen and work from morning to night.

One of the things the poor child had to do was to go twice a day and fetch water from a spring a good half-mile away from their house and bring it home in a big pitcher. One day, when she was at the spring, a poor woman came up and begged for a drink.

'Of course, good mother,' the girl answered her. She rinsed her pitcher at once and filled it with water from the fountain-head where it was clearest. Then she offered it to the old woman, holding the pitcher for her to drink more easily.

When the old woman had finished drinking she said to her: 'You are so pretty, and you have been so sweet and kind, that I cannot resist giving you a present.' (The old woman was really a fairy who had disguised herself as a poor peasant woman in order to test the girl's goodness.)

'The gift I will give you,' the fairy went on more, 'is that at every word you speak a flower or a precious stone shall fall from your lips.'

When the pretty girl reached home her mother scolded her for being so long coming back from the spring.

'I am sorry to have been so long, Mother,' said the poor girl, and as she spoke, there dropped from her lips three roses, three pearls and three enormous diamonds.

'Am I seeing things,' said her mother in amazement, 'or did I really see pearls and diamonds fall from her mouth? What has happened to you, daughter dear?'

She had never spoken to her kindly before.

The poor child innocently told her all that had befallen her, scattering a great many diamonds in the process.

'Indeed,' said the mother, 'I must send my other girl. Come here, Fanny, and see what falls from your sister's lips when she speaks. Wouldn't you like to have the same gift? All you have to do is go and draw water from the spring and when a poor woman comes along and asks you for a drink, give it to her like a good girl.'

'Me, go to the spring? I don't think!' retorted the spoilt girl.

'I tell you to go,' repeated her mother, 'and quick about it.'

The girl went, still grumbling, and taking with her the best silver jug in the house. No sooner had she reached the spring than she saw a splendidly dressed lady come out of the wood and ask her for a drink. It was the same fairy who had appeared to her sister, but she had put on the dress and manners of a princess to test the girl's ill nature.

'Do you think I have come here only to give you a drink?' said the conceited girl rudely. 'I suppose I've brought this silver jug on purpose for your ladyship to drink from? That's likely, I must say! Drink from the spring if you want to.'

'That is not very kind of you,' said the fairy mildly. 'Well, since you are so ungracious, the gift I shall give you is that whenever you open your mouth to speak a snake or a toad shall pop out.'

The moment her mother set eyes on the girl she cried out: 'Well, my girl?'

'Well, Mother?' replied the spoilt girl crossly, spitting out a toad and an adder as she spoke.

'Oh, heavens!' shrieked her mother, 'what has gone wrong? It is all your sister's fault. I'll make her pay for it!'

She hurried off to beat her there and then, but the poor child ran away and hid herself in the near-by forest.

There the king's son found her as he was on his way home from hunting. He asked what such a pretty girl was doing all by herself and what she was crying for.

'Alas, Sir,' she said, 'my mother has driven me away from home.'

The king's son, seeing five or six pearls and as many diamonds fall from her lips, begged her to tell him how this came about. She told him the whole story. The king's son quite fell in love with her and, reckoning that such a gift was worth more than all the dowries other brides could bring him, he took her back to the king his father's palace and married her.

As for her sister, she made herself so thoroughly disliked that even her own mother drove her out. The poor thing wandered about without finding anyone willing to take her in, until at last she curled up in a corner of the woods and died.

Cinderella
or
the little glass slipper

Once upon a time there was a gentleman whose second wife was the proudest and haughtiest woman imaginable. She had two daughters exactly like herself who took after her in every way. Her husband had one young daughter of his own, but she was a creature of matchless goodness and gentleness. She inherited this from her mother who had been the sweetest woman in the world.

The wedding was no sooner over than the stepmother began to show her evil temper. She could not bear the other child's goodness because it made her own daughters seem more unpleasant than ever by comparison.

She made her do all the most menial chores about the house. It was she who had to wash the dishes, scrub the steps, and clean both my lady's chamber and those of her stuck-up daughters. She slept on an old straw mattress in a garret right at the top of the house, while in her sisters' rooms the floors were parquet, the beds the latest thing, and they had mirrors in which they could see themselves from top to toe.

The poor girl bore it all patiently. She dared not complain to her father because he was entirely ruled by his wife and would only have scolded her. When she had finished her work she would sit huddled in the chimney corner among the cinders, and so it was that she came to be known as Cinderpuss. The younger of her stepsisters, who was not quite as rude as the elder, called her Cinderella. Even so, for all her ragged clothes, Cinderella was still a hundred times lovelier than her sisters, no matter how splendidly they dressed.

A time came when the king's son was to give a ball, to which

everyone who was anyone was invited. Naturally the two young ladies were asked, since they were very much a part of the fashionable world in that country. They were highly delighted, and very busy selecting their most becoming dresses and hair-styles.

For Cinderella the ball only meant more work, ironing and pressing her sisters' finery and goffering their ruffled sleeves. They could talk of nothing but what they were going to wear.

'I,' said the elder, 'shall wear my red velvet dress, with the English lace collar.'

'I,' said the younger, 'have only my everyday underskirt, but to make up for it I shall wear my gown with the gold flowers, and my diamonds, which are not to be sniffed at.'

They sent for the most fashionable hairdresser to arrange their elaborately frilled caps and bought patches from the best shop.

They called in Cinderella, who had excellent taste, and asked her advice. She gave them the best in the world and even offered to do their hair for them, an offer they were very glad to accept.

While she was dressing their hair her stepsisters said to her:

'Cinderella, wouldn't you like to go to the ball?'

'Oh ladies, you are making fun of me. Such things are not for me.'

'You are quite right there. How people would laugh to see a Cinderpuss going to the ball!'

Anyone but Cinderella would have left their hair in a tangle, but she was a kind-hearted girl and arranged their hair to perfection.

They were so overcome with excitement that for nearly two days they could not eat a thing. They broke over a dozen laces pulling in their stays to give themselves smaller waists, and were for ever in front of a mirror.

At last the great day came. Off they went, and Cinderella gazed after them until they were well out of sight. When she could not see them any longer, she began to cry.

Seeing her in tears, her godmother asked her what was the matter.

'I wish – oh, I do so wish –'

She was sobbing so hard she could not even finish, but her god-mother was a fairy and so she said:

'You wish you could go to the ball, is that it?'

'Oh, yes,' sighed Cinderella.

'Very well,' said her godmother, 'if you'll be a good girl, I'll see to it that you go.'

She took Cinderella indoors and said to her:

'Run into the garden and fetch me a pumpkin.'

Cinderella went at once and picked the biggest she could find and brought it to her godmother, although she could not imagine how a pumpkin could help her to get to the ball.

Her godmother scooped out the inside and when only the rind was left she touched it with her wand. In an instant, the pumpkin was turned into a handsome golden coach.

Then she went and looked in the mouse-trap, where she found

six mice, all alive. She told Cinderella to lift the gate of the trap a little, and as each mouse came out she gave it a touch with her wand which immediately turned it into a splendid horse. This made a fine team of six dappled mouse-grey horses.

But she was hard put to it to think of something to turn into a coachman, until Cinderella said: 'I'll go and see if there is a rat in the rat-trap. We could make a coachman of him.'

'So we could,' agreed her godmother, 'go and see.'

Cinderella brought her the rat-trap with three big rats in it.

The fairy chose the one with the most impressive whiskers and transformed him at a touch of her wand into a portly coachman with the finest moustaches ever seen. Next she said: 'Go into the garden and bring me the six lizards you will find behind the water butt.'

She had no sooner brought them than her godmother turned them into six footmen in splendid liveries who immediately sprang up behind the coach as though they had done nothing else all their lives. Then the fairy said to Cinderella: 'Well, that is how you can go to the ball! Aren't you pleased?'

'Oh, yes, but how can I got like this, in my old, worn-out clothes?'

Her godmother merely touched her lightly with her wand and in an instant her ragged dress was changed into a gown of cloth of gold and silver, all sewn with precious stones. Then she gave her a pair of the prettiest little glass slippers in the world.

So, splendidly dressed, Cinderella climbed into her coach. Her godmother told her, above all, not to stay beyond midnight,

warning her that if she lingered at the ball one moment longer, her coach would turn back into a pumpkin, her horses into mice, her footmen into lizards and her clothes become again the rags they had been before.

Cinderella promised her godmother faithfully to leave the ball before midnight, and set off, beside herself with happiness.

The king's son was told that a great princess had arrived whom nobody knew, and hurried out to welcome her. It was the prince himself who handed her from her coach and led her into the ballroom.

A sudden hush fell on the room. The dancing ceased, the violins stopped playing and everyone gazed in wonder at the beautiful stranger. The only sound was a confused murmur of: 'Oh, how beautiful she is.'

Even the king, old man though he was, could not help looking at her, and remarked privately to the queen that it was a long time since he had seen such an attractive-looking girl.

All the ladies were busy studying her dress and her hair, with a view to having the same things themselves the next day, if they could only find such gorgeous stuffs and such clever dressmakers.

The prince placed her in the seat of honour, and claimed her for the next dance. She danced with such grace that everyone admired her more than ever.

A magnificent supper was served, but the prince was so taken up with gazing at Cinderella that he ate nothing at all.

She went and sat by her sisters and treated them with great kindness, sharing with them the oranges and lemons the prince had given her. They were very surprised at this, because they had not recognized her.

While they were talking, Cinderella heard the clock striking a quarter to twelve. At once she rose and, with a deep curtsy to the assembled company, hurried away as fast as she could.

When she reached home she went straight to her godmother and thanked her. Then she told her how much she would like to go to the ball the next day, because the king's son had asked her. She was still describing to her godmother all that had happened at the ball when her two sisters knocked on the door. Cinderella went to open it for them.

'What a long time you've been coming home,' she said, rubbing her eyes and stretching as if she had only just woken up. In fact she had not felt the least bit sleepy since she had seen them last.

'You would not have had a dull moment if you had come to the ball,' one of her sisters told her. 'There was the most beautiful princess there, the most beautiful you could possibly imagine. She was particularly nice to us, and she gave us oranges and lemons.'

Cinderella was highly delighted. She asked the princess's name, but they told her no one knew it, and the king's son was nearly in despair and would give anything in the world to know who she was.

Cinderella smiled and said: 'She must have been truly lovely. Oh, goodness, how lucky you are! Couldn't I go and see her? Oh, dear Javotte, please lend me your everyday yellow dress.'

'I should think not indeed!' said Javotte. 'Lend my dress to a nasty little Cinderpuss like you! I'd be out of my mind.'

This refusal was just what Cinderella had been expecting, and she was quite content with it because she would have been in a pretty pickle if her sister *had* offered to lend her the dress.

The next day the two sisters went to the ball, and so did Cinderella, dressed even more splendidly than before. The king's son never left her side and plied her with endless pretty compliments.

Young Cinderella was enjoying herself so much that she quite forgot what her godmother had told her. The result was that she heard the first stroke of midnight chime when she had thought it was not yet eleven. She jumped up and fled as swiftly as a deer.

The prince followed, but he could not catch her. However, she did lose one of her glass slippers, and very carefully the prince picked it up.

Cinderella arrived home panting, without her coach or her footmen, dressed in her ragged old clothes. All that remained of her finery was one tiny glass slipper, the pair to the one she had lost.

The guards at the palace gate were asked if they had seen a princess leaving, but they said the only person who had gone out was a little ragged girl who looked more like a peasant than a princess.

When her two sisters came home from the ball, Cinderella asked if they had enjoyed themselves again, and whether the beautiful lady had been there. They told her she was, but had run away on the stroke of midnight in such a hurry that she had left behind one of her little glass slippers, the prettiest thing imaginable. The king's son had picked it up and had done nothing but gaze at it for the rest of the ball. There was no doubt that he was very much in love with the little slipper's beautiful owner.

They spoke the truth. A few days later the king's son sent out trumpeters to proclaim that he would marry the lady whose foot fitted the slipper exactly.

It was tried first on the princesses, then on the duchesses, and so on throughout the whole court, but all in vain.

At last it came to the house where the two sisters lived. They did their best to cram their feet into the slipper, but they could not manage it.

Cinderella was watching them and recognized her slipper.

'Let me see if it will fit me,' she laughed.

Her sisters shouted with derisive laughter, but the gentleman who was trying on the slipper looked closely at Cinderella and, deciding that she was very lovely, he said that this was only right, as his instructions were to try the slipper on every single girl. He made Cinderella sit down and when he lifted the slipper to her little foot he saw it slip on easily and fit as though it had been moulded in wax.

Her sisters had the shock of their lives, but they were still more amazed when Cinderella drew the other little slipper out of her pocket and put it on.

At that moment the fairy godmother appeared and with a stroke of her wand made Cinderella's clothes more splendid than ever before.

Then her two sisters knew her for the beautiful lady they had seen at the ball. They threw themselves at her feet and begged her to forgive them for all their unkindness. Cinderella raised them up and kissed them, telling them she forgave them with all her heart and hoped they would always love her. She was escorted back to the young prince, dressed in her beautiful new clothes, and he thought her lovelier than ever. A few days later they were married.

Cinderella was as good as she was beautiful and she brought her two sisters to live in the palace, and they were married on the self-same day to two great lords at the court.

Riquet with the quiff

Once upon a time there was a queen who had a son so ugly and misshapen that for a good while people could scarcely believe he was human. A fairy who happened to be there when he was born promised that he should be very very clever, and even added that she would grant him the power of making the person he loved best as clever as himself.

This comforted the poor queen a little, for she was terribly distressed to have brought such a hideous little thing into the world.

True enough, the child had no sooner begun to speak than he was saying any number of witty things, and everything he did showed such intelligence that no one could resist him.

I forgot to say that the boy was born with a little quiff of hair on top of his head and because of this people called him Riquet with the Quiff, Riquet being his family name.

Seven or eight years later, the queen of a neighbouring country gave birth to twin daughters. The first to come into the world was lovelier than the day is long, and the queen was so delighted with her that it was feared excessive joy might do her some harm.

The same fairy who had been present when little Riquet with the Quiff was born happened to be there, and to calm the queen's excitement she told her roundly that the little princess should have no brains at all and would be as silly as she was beautiful.

The queen was bitterly disappointed, but a few moments later she had an even worse shock. Her second daughter was extremely ugly.

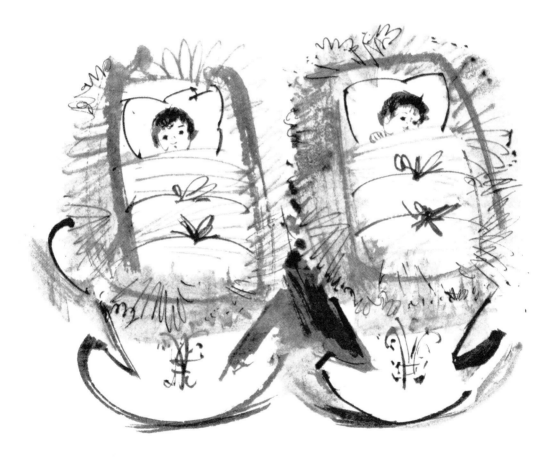

'Do not distress yourself so, my lady,' said the fairy. 'Your daughter shall make up for it in other ways. She shall be so clever that people will scarcely notice that she is not very pretty.'

'Heaven grant it may be so,' said the queen, 'but is there no way of giving the elder, who is so beautiful, just a little sense?'

'I can do nothing for her in the way of sense, my lady,' the fairy said, 'but as far as beauty goes anything is within my power, and since I would do anything to make you happy I shall give her the gift of being able to make the person she loves as beautiful as herself.'

As the two princesses grew up, so their virtues grew with them, until everyone was talking about how lovely the elder was and how clever the younger.

Admittedly, their defects also increased a good deal as they

grew older. The younger grew visibly plainer and plainer, while the elder became more stupid every day. If anyone asked her a question, she either had no answer at all or else she said something silly, and as if that were not enough she was so clumsy that she could not put four pieces of china on the mantelpiece without breaking one, or drink a glass of water without spilling half of it over her dress. Needless to say, in spite of the advantage good looks can be to a girl, the younger twin was nearly always more popular than her sister. People were attracted by the prettier one at first and liked to look at her and admire her beauty, but they very soon deserted her for the clever one, who was much better company. In less than fifteen minutes she would be left quite alone while everyone crowded round her younger sister.

The elder princess was not too stupid to see what was happening and would willingly have parted with all her beauty for half her sister's wit.

The queen was a sensible woman, but even she could not help sometimes blaming the girl for her silliness, and this made the poor princess ready to die of misery.

One day when she had run away into the woods to cry over her troubles she saw a little man coming towards her. He was magnificently dressed but quite horribly ugly.

It was young prince Riquet with the Quiff. He had fallen in love with her portrait which had travelled all over the world, and had left his father's kingdom to enjoy the pleasure of seeing and talking to her.

Delighted to come upon her alone in this way, he introduced himself very politely and with all the respect imaginable. But when he had paid her the usual compliments he noticed that she seemed very unhappy.

'I cannot understand, my lady,' he said, 'how anyone as lovely as you are can possibly be as sad as you appear to be. Although I can boast of having seen a great many lovely ladies, I may say that I have seen none whose loveliness compares with yours.'

'You are pleased to say so, sir,' answered the princess, and that was all.

'Beauty is such a blessing,' Riquet went on, 'that it can take the place of everything else, and if you have that I do not see that anything can trouble you very much.'

'I would rather be as ugly as you,' said the princess, 'and be clever, than as pretty as I am and such a fool.'

'My lady, there is no greater proof of wit than the belief that one lacks it. It is perfectly natural that the more sense a person has, the less they believe they possess.'

'I don't know about that,' said the princess, 'but I do know that I am very stupid, and that is what is making me so miserable I could die.'

'If that is all that is troubling you, my lady, I can easily put an end to your unhappiness.'

'How can you do that?' asked the princess.

'It is in my power, my lady,' Riquet with the Quiff told her, 'to make the person I love most as clever as can be, and since you, my lady, are that person, it is up to you whether you will

105

become as clever as you could wish – only you must be prepared to marry me.'

The princess was too astonished to say a word.

'I see that my proposal offends you,' said Riquet, 'and I can quite understand it. But I will give you a whole year to think it over.'

The princess was such a scatterbrain and so longed to be intelligent that it seemed to her the end of the year would never come, and so of course she accepted Riquet's proposal.

She had no sooner promised Riquet with the Quiff that she

107

would marry him in a year to the day, than she suddenly felt a completely different person. She found it incredibly easy to say anything she wanted to, and in the most lively, clear and natural manner. She immediately began a brilliantly witty conversation with Riquet and talked with such spirit that he began to wonder if he had not made her cleverer than he was himself.

When she went back to the palace the whole court was at a loss to understand this sudden, remarkable transformation. For every unfortunate remark she had made before, the princess now had something to say that was neatly put and very much to the point.

The whole court was overjoyed. Only the younger sister was not best pleased, because now that she no longer had the advantage of intelligence she seemed a dismal, unattractive little thing beside her sister.

The king took to asking his elder daughter's advice, and sometimes even held his council of state in her apartments.

The news of the change in the princess spread far and wide, and young princes came from all the neighbouring kingdoms to pay court to her. Nearly all of them asked for her hand in marriage, but she thought them all rather dull and heard them out without falling the least bit in love with any of them.

At last one came who was so rich and powerful, so handsome and intelligent, that the princess could not help liking him.

When her father noticed this, he told her she was free to choose her own husband, and she had only to tell him her choice.

Now the more sense a person has, the more complicated a

109

decision of this kind becomes, so the princess thanked her father and asked for time to think it over.

It so happened that the place she chose to go and think quietly over what she had to do was the very wood in which she had first met Riquet with the Quiff.

As she was walking along, deep in thought, she heard a muffled sound under her feet as though a great many people were rushing about. The princess listened more carefully and heard a voice say: 'Bring me that boiler.' Then another: 'Put some wood on the fire.'

At the same time the earth opened and she saw at her feet what looked like a huge kitchen filled with cooks and scullions and all the other people needed for preparing a great banquet. Out came a band of some twenty or thirty cooks and set up a long table in a woodland ride. They all gathered round it, and set to work trussing and basting for all they were worth, singing together as they worked.

The princess was astonished at the sight and asked them for whom they worked.

'We serve prince Riquet with the Quiff, my lady,' replied their leader, 'and tomorrow is his wedding.'

The princess was more surprised than ever. She remembered suddenly that it was a year ago to the day that she had promised to marry prince Riquet with the Quiff and she felt as though the ground had been swept from under her. The reason she had not remembered her promise was that when she made it she had still been a fool, and the new intelligence Riquet had given

110

her had made her forget all the silly things she had done before.

She had not gone another thirty yards before Riquet himself appeared before her, dressed with all the splendour and magnificence of a prince on his wedding day.

'My lady,' he said, 'you see me here true to my word, and I do not doubt that you have come to keep yours and make me the happiest of men by giving me your hand in marriage.'

'To tell you the truth,' answered the princess, 'I have not yet made up my mind about that, but I fear I shall never be able to decide as you would wish.'

'You amaze me, my lady,' said Riquet with the Quiff.

'I know I must do so,' said the princess, 'and certainly if I had to deal with a crude and insensitive man I should be in a very awkward position. He would tell me that a princess must be bound by her word and that I must marry him as I had promised. But since I am talking to the most understanding man in the world, I know he will listen to reason. You know that even when I was only a fool I still could not bring myself to marry you. Now you have made me clever and consequently still harder to please, so how can you expect me to make a decision today which I could not do then? If you really wanted to marry me you made a great mistake in curing me of my stupidity and making me see things more clearly than I did then.'

'If, as you say, a heartless man would have the right to reproach you for breaking your word,' said Riquet, 'do you seriously expect me not to do the same, my lady, when my whole life's happiness is at stake? Is it right for a reasonable man to suffer more than an unreasonable one? Can you seriously believe that, when you are so reasonable yourself, and desired reason so much? But let us consider the facts, if you please. Apart from my ugliness, is there something about me you dislike? Are you dissatisfied with my birth or intelligence, my manners or my temper?'

'Not in the least,' the princess told him, 'in fact I like all the things about you which you have mentioned very much indeed.'

'Then if that is the case,' said Riquet, 'I shall be happy because it is in your power to make me the most agreeable of men.'

'How can I do that?' asked the princess.

'You can do it,' Riquet answered, 'if you love me enough
to wish it may be so. If you doubt this, my lady, you must know
that the same fairy who gave me, when I was born, the power
of making the person I loved clever, also gave you the gift of
making the man you love handsome. If you want to, you can do
this.'

'If that is true,' said the princess, 'then I wish with all my
heart for you to be the handsomest and nicest prince in the world.
Any power I have, I give to you.'

No sooner had the princess said these words than Riquet with the Quiff seemed to her the handsomest man in the world, the most elegant and attractive prince she had ever set eyes on.

There are those who say that this was nothing to do with the fairy's spells, but that love alone had worked the transformation. They say that when the princess thought about her lover's

wisdom and perseverance and all the virtues of his mind and character, she no longer saw his crooked body and ugly face, that the hump on his back seemed merely the natural stance of a man of the world, and the dreadful limp she had noticed before now struck her as no more than a slight, attractive stoop. They will have it that to her his eyes twinkled more brightly for their squint and that his cross-eyed expression was due to the agonies of love, and that even his big red nose looked martial and heroic to her. However that may be, the princess promised to marry him at once, provided he obtained the king her father's consent.

116

The king already knew Riquet with the Quiff to be a good and wise prince, and when he heard of his daughter's regard for him, he was delighted to welcome him as a son-in-law.

The wedding took place the next day, just as Riquet with the Quiff had meant it to, with all the celebrations he had planned so long before.

Tom Thumb

Once upon a time there lived a woodcutter and his wife who had seven children, all of them boys. The eldest was only ten and the youngest seven. People wondered how the woodcutter came to have so many children in such a short time, but this was because his wife was a quick worker and never had less than two at once.

They were very poor, and their seven children were a great burden to them because none of them was yet able to earn his own living. But it was their youngest child that worried them most of all. He was very delicate and never spoke a word, and they took for stupidity what was really a sign of good sense. He was very tiny, and when he was born had been hardly bigger than a man's thumb; for this reason he was called Tom Thumb.

This poor child was the butt of the entire family and got the blame for everything. All the same, he was quicker and brighter than his brothers, and although he did not say very much he kept his ears open.

One very bad year, the family were so close to starvation that the poor people made up their minds to get rid of their children.

One night, as the woodcutter was sitting by the fire with his wife after the children were in bed, he said to her, his heart heavy with grief:

'We both know we can no longer feed our family but I cannot watch them die of hunger before my eyes. I have made up my mind to take them into the woods tomorrow and lose them. It will be easy enough. All we have to do is slip away without being seen while they are busy looking for firewood.'

120

'Oh,' cried his wife, 'do you mean to say you could take your own children out and lose them?'

Her husband pleaded their terrible poverty, but it was no good. She could not agree. Poor she might be, but she was their mother. In the end, however, the thought of the grief it would cause her to see them die of hunger made her give way, and she went weeping to bed.

Now little Tom Thumb had heard everything that was said. Hearing from his bed that they were talking about something very serious, he had got up very quietly and crept underneath his father's stool to listen without being seen. He went back to bed and lay awake all the rest of the night, thinking about what he must do. In the morning he got up very early and went down to the edge of the stream. There he filled his pockets with little white stones, and then went back to the house.

Off they went and Tom Thumb said nothing to his brothers about what he knew.

They went into a forest so thick that they could not see one another more than ten paces apart. The woodcutter began chopping wood while the children collected twigs to bundle into faggots. Seeing them hard at work, their father and mother began to move gradually farther away and then suddenly ran off down a small path.

When the children saw that they were all alone they began to bawl and shout as hard as they could. Tom Thumb let them cry, although he knew very well how to find the way home because he had been dropping the little white stones out of his pocket all the way as they walked along. At last he told them:

'Don't be frightened, brothers. Mother and Father have left us here, but I will get you home safely. Just follow me.'

They all followed behind as he led them back along the same paths by which they had come into the forest, all the way back to their cottage. At first they dared not go in, but all crowded round the door to listen to what their parents were saying.

123

Now the woodcutter and his wife had no sooner reached home than the lord of the village sent them ten crowns, which he had owed them for so long that they had despaired of ever seeing the money. The poor souls were half dead with hunger and this put new life into them. The woodcutter sent his wife straight out to the butcher. It was so long since they had had anything to eat that she bought three times as much meat as they needed to make a meal for two people.

When they had eaten their fill, the woodcutter's wife said:

'Oh dear, oh dear, where are our poor children now? What we have left over would have made a good meal for them. And anyway, William, it was your idea to lose them. I told you we should be sorry. What are they doing now in that forest? Oh dear, oh goodness, perhaps the wolves have eaten them already! Oh, what a monster you are to lose your own children like that.'

At last the woodcutter lost patience. If she told him once she told him twenty times that he would be sorry and had gone on to such an extent that in the end he threatened to beat her if she did not hold her tongue.

It was not that the woodcutter was not just as upset as his wife, maybe even more so; but she was nagging him unmercifully and, like a good many other people, he liked a woman to talk sense but found one who was always saying 'I told you so' very irritating indeed.

The woodcutter's wife was sobbing bitterly.

'Oh deary me,' she wailed, 'where are my children now, all my poor little boys?'

125

At last she said it so loudly that the children who were standing outside the door heard her, and they all began shouting at once: 'Here we are! Here we are!'

She rushed to open the door for them and gathered them into her arms, crying:

'My darlings, how glad I am to see you again! You look worn out and you must be dreadfully hungry. And you, Peter, just look at the mess you're in! Come here and let me clean you up.'

Peter was her eldest boy and she loved him best of all her children because he was a little bit of a redhead, just like herself.

They sat down to table and ate so heartily that it warmed their parents' hearts to see them, all talking at once about how frightened they had been in the forest.

The good people were delighted to have their children back with them and their happiness lasted just as long as the ten crowns. But when the money was spent they were as miserable as before, and made up their minds to lose them again. Only this time, to make quite sure, they meant to take them much, much farther. But they could not talk about their plans secretly enough to escape Tom Thumb's sharp ears, and he made up his mind to save them all as he had done before. But when he got up very early in the morning to go and collect some little stones, he found the house door firmly locked and could not get out.

He could not think what to do. Then the woodcutter's wife gave them each a piece of bread for their lunch and he had the idea of using his bread instead of pebbles by crumbling it along the path as they went. He tucked it safely into his pocket.

Their father and mother took them into the deepest, darkest part of the forest and when they were there they slipped away through the trees and left them. This did not worry Tom Thumb very much because he thought he would easily be able to find the way back by the bread he had dropped everywhere as he walked. He had a nasty shock when he could not find so much as a crumb. The birds had come and eaten it all.

Now they were in a dreadful plight. The farther they walked, the more lost they became and the deeper they plunged into the forest. As darkness came, a great wind got up and frightened them horribly. They imagined every noise around them was made by howling wolves coming to eat them up, and scarcely dared to speak or move their heads.

Then it began to pour with rain and they were soon soaked to the skin. They slithered at every step and fell down in the mud and clambered out covered in mud from head to foot.

Tom Thumb climbed a tree to see what he could see. Craning his neck in all directions, he saw a tiny glimmer of light, like a candle, far away in the forest. He clambered down from the tree but was disappointed to find that from the ground he could see nothing at all.

However, he and his brothers set off in the direction in which he had seen the light, and after walking for some time they broke clear of the trees and saw it again. Even so they had a good

many frights and often lost sight of it because it disappeared every time there was a dip in the ground, but at last they came to the house where the candle was burning.

They knocked on the door and a woman came and opened it. She asked them what they wanted.

Tom Thumb told her they were poor children who had lost their way in the forest and begged her to give them a bed for the night. The woman looked at the seven pretty children and burst into tears.

'Oh, my poor children,' she said, 'what a place you have come

to. Don't you know this house belongs to an ogre who eats little children?'

Tom Thumb was shaking like a leaf, and so were all his brothers. 'Oh, please, ma'am,' he said, 'what are we to do? If you will not take us in, the wolves in the forest will certainly eat us, and if you don't mind we would prefer to be eaten by his honour the ogre. After all, he may have pity on us, if you were to ask him nicely.'

Thinking that she would be able to hide them from her husband until the next morning, the ogre's wife let them in and sat them down to warm themselves by a huge fire where a whole sheep was roasting on a spit for the ogre's supper.

Just as they were beginning to get warm they heard three or four hefty thumps on the door. It was the ogre coming home. His wife at once hid them under the bed and went to open the door.

The ogre's first question was whether his dinner was ready and his wine drawn. Then he sat down at the table. The mutton was still red and raw but he liked it all the better for that. He sniffed to left and right, saying he could smell human flesh.

'It must be the veal I am dressing that you can smell,' said his wife.

'I can smell human flesh, I tell you,' the ogre repeated, looking suspiciously at his wife, 'and there is something here I don't understand.'

With these words he got up from the table and went straight over to the bed.

'Aha!' he said. 'So this is how you try and deceive me, you wicked woman! I've half a mind to eat you too, so think yourself lucky you're such a stringy old bird! Now three ogre friends of mine are coming to visit me one of these days and this little bag of game will come in very handy.' One after another he hauled the boys out from under the bed.

The poor children fell on their knees and begged for mercy but they were dealing with the cruellest ogre of all. Far from taking pity on them, he was already licking his lips and telling his wife what tasty morsels they would make when she served them up with a good sauce.

He went to fetch his big knife and advanced on the poor children, sharpening it on a long stone in his left hand as he came.

He had already taken hold of one of them when his wife said:

'What do you want to do it now for? Surely you'll have time enough tomorrow?'

'Quiet, woman,' said the ogre. 'They'll be all the better for hanging a little.'

'But you have such a lot of meat already,' his wife went on. 'Look, a calf, two sheep and half a pig.'

'You're right there,' the ogre agreed. 'Well, give them a good supper so that they don't get thin, and then put them to bed.'

The good woman was overjoyed and brought them a delicious

supper, but the boys were too frightened to eat. As for the ogre, he went back to his wine, feeling very happy to have such a splendid feast to offer his friends. He drank a dozen more cups than usual and was then forced to go to bed with a slight headache.

Now the ogre had seven daughters, not yet grown up. These little ogresses all had the most lovely complexions because they ate nothing but fresh meat like their father, but they had little round grey eyes, hooked noses and enormous mouths with very long, sharp teeth set very wide apart. They were not so very wicked as yet, but they promised well because they were already fond of biting little babies to suck their blood.

They had been put to bed early and all seven of them were lying in one big bed, each with a golden crown on her head. There was another bed the same size in the room and it was here that the ogre's wife put the seven boys to sleep. After that she herself lay down beside her husband.

Tom Thumb had noticed that the ogre's daughters all had golden crowns on their heads. Suspecting that the ogre might regret not having killed them all that night, he got up in the middle of the night and took off his own and his brother's caps. Then he crept over very quietly and put them on the heads of the ogre's seven daughters, having first taken their golden crowns to put on himself and his six brothers. He did this so that the ogre would mistake them for his daughters and his own daughters for the little boys he meant to murder.

Everything fell out just as he had planned. The ogre woke up at midnight and felt sorry he had put off until tomorrow what he might have done today. He jumped quickly out of bed and fetched his big knife.

'Let's see how those little rascals are,' he said 'once and for all.'

He felt his way up to his daughters' room and went up to the bed where the little boys were fast asleep, all except Tom Thumb. He was very frightened when he felt the ogre's big hand touch his head, as it had touched all his brothers'.

When the ogre felt the golden crowns he said to himself: 'Upon my word, I nearly made a nasty mistake. I can see I must have had too much to drink last night.'

Then he went over to his daughters' bed and felt the little boys' caps.

'Ah, here they are!' he said. 'The little dears! Now for it!'

With these words he chopped off the heads of all seven little ogresses in a moment. Then he went back to bed beside his wife, feeling very pleased with his night's work.

As soon as Tom Thumb heard the ogre snoring he woke up his brothers and told them to get dressed quickly and follow him. They went quietly down into the garden and jumped over the

wall. Then they ran as hard as they could nearly all night, shaking
with fear and with no idea where they were going.

When the ogre woke up he said to his wife: 'Go upstairs and
dress those little rascals who were here last night.'

The ogre's wife was very surprised at her husband's kindness.
She had no idea what he meant by dressing them and thought
he was telling her to help them put on their clothes. She went
upstairs and was horrified to see her seven daughters all with
their throats cut, swimming in blood. The first thing she did

was to faint, which is what most women would do in the same circumstances.

Thinking that his wife would take too long over the job he had given her, the ogre soon went upstairs to help her. He was just as astonished as his wife at the fearful sight that met his eyes.

'What have I done?' he cried. 'Those little wretches shall pay for this when I catch them.'

Throwing a jug of water over his wife's face to revive her, he ordered: 'Give me my seven-league boots, quickly, and I'll go and catch them.'

He rushed outside and scoured the countryside until he came to the road the poor children had taken. They were not more than a hundred yards from their father's cottage when they saw the ogre striding over mountains and crossing rivers as easily as if they had been tiny streams.

Seeing a hollow rock close by, Tom Thumb told his brothers to hide inside. Then he went in himself, still watching what the ogre was doing.

Now the ogre was feeling very tired after his long, fruitless journey (because seven-league boots are very tiring to the feet) and he wanted a rest. As luck would have it, he came and sat down on the very rock where the little boys were hiding. He was so tired that when he had sat there for a little while he fell asleep and started snoring so dreadfully that the poor children were every bit as scared as they had been when he was brandishing his huge knife to cut their throats.

Tom Thumb was not so frightened as his brothers, and told

141

them to run away home quickly while the ogre was fast asleep and not to worry about him. They did as he told them and were soon safe inside.

Going up to the ogre, Tom Thumb gently drew off his boots and put them on himself. The boots were very large but, being magic, they had the power of growing larger or smaller to fit whoever put them on, so that they fitted Tom's feet as though they had been made for him.

He went straight to the ogre's house where he found the ogre's wife weeping over her murdered daughters.

'Your husband is in terrible danger,' Tom Thumb told her. 'He has been captured by a gang of robbers who have sworn to kill him unless he gives them all his gold and silver. They were actually holding a dagger to his throat when he saw me and begged me to come and warn you of his plight and tell you to hand over all his treasure. You must keep nothing back because if you do they will kill him without mercy. The matter is so urgent that he told me to wear his seven-league boots, as you can see, to save time and also so that you would believe I was not an impostor.'

The good woman was scared out of her wits and at once gave him everything she had, because the ogre was a good husband even though he did like eating little children.

Tom Thumb made his way back to his father's cottage, loaded with all the ogre's wealth, and was given a joyful welcome.

There are many people who do not altogether agree about this last part of the story and say that Tom Thumb never robbed

142

the ogre, and that the only reason he had no scruples about taking the seven-league boots was because the ogre only used them to chase little children.

Their story is that they know this for a fact because they have actually been to dinner in the woodcutter's house. They say that when Tom Thumb had put on the ogre's boots, he went to the court where he knew everyone was very worried about the outcome of a battle which had been fought against an army two hundred leagues away. They say he went to the king and

told him that if he liked he would go and bring back news of the army before nightfall. The king promised him a great deal of money if he could do so.

Tom Thumb brought the news the same night, and after this first exploit his fame spread so far that he could earn as much money as he wanted. The king paid him handsomely for taking orders to the army, but he earned a great deal more from ladies who would give him anything he wanted to bring them news of their lovers. There were a few ladies, too, who gave him letters for their husbands, but they paid him so badly and what he earned in this way brought him in so little that it scarcely counted.

When Tom Thumb had acted as courier for some time and amassed a great deal of money, he went back to his father's house where he was welcomed with more delight than one could possibly imagine.

He set up his whole family in comfort, bought newly created posts for his father and brothers, and so they all lived happily ever after, not forgetting Tom himself.

Patient Griselda

At the foot of the mighty mountains where the river Po emerges from its beds of reeds and flows out into the open country, there once lived a gallant young prince, the darling of his land. He seemed formed by heaven to combine all the rarest gifts of body and mind, gifts in general bestowed but sparingly even on great kings.

He was strong and agile, a born warrior and yet with an instinctive passion for the arts. He loved fighting and victory and all the great and valorous deeds which make a grand name in history, but his generous, affectionate heart rejoiced still more in the lasting glory of making his people happy.

Unfortunately his noble nature was overcast by one sombre cloud: a melancholy temper which made him believe in his heart of hearts that all women were false and faithless. To him, even the rarest and best of women seemed to be hypocrites, proud and haughty, bitter enemies whose one ambition was to dominate the wretched men in their power.

It is a fact that the husbands and wives he saw around him did nothing to remove his hatred, and the result was that he swore more than once that he would never marry, not even if heaven, which had showered him with blessings, should offer him the most wonderful wife imaginable.

The prince generally devoted the mornings to his royal business, dealing wisely with all the problems of government, protecting helpless widows and orphans and abolishing taxes which has been introduced to pay the cost of some bygone war. Then he would spend the rest of the day hunting bears or wild boar which, however fierce, could never frighten him half as much as the fair sex, whose company he fled.

His subjects, however, were extremely anxious to have an heir who might one day rule them just as kindly, and they were always begging the prince to give them a son. One day they all came to the palace in a body to make one last effort. A very learned man who was the greatest orator of those times did his utmost to impress the prince with their desire to see him found a dynasty, and so ensure the prosperity of his people. He even

wound up his speech with a reference to a new star that should outshine the moon itself.

The prince answered them very quietly and simply: 'I am grateful for your eagerness to see me married. It shows your love for me and I am deeply touched. I wish I could grant your wish tomorrow, but in my view marriage is a matter in which any sensible man will tread very cautiously. Look at all the young girls you see, all virtue and goodness and modest sincerity when they are at home with their families, yet they are no sooner married than they throw off their disguise. Once settled in their own households they think they can do just as they please, with no more need to be good.

'One will turn into a bad-tempered scold, always shouting and complaining, another become a flirt and be always chattering and gossiping, and yet another suddenly develop an intense passion for the arts and grow into a critical, opinionated blue-stocking. And another will set herself up as a gambler and lose all her money, rings, furniture and valuables, and even her clothes, at cards.

'But however different they may be, as I see it there is only one thing they all like, and that is to have their own way. Now I believe that married people can only live happily together when the man is master in his own house, and so, if you want me to marry, you must find me a beautiful young girl who has no pride or vanity, one who is utterly obedient, of proven patience and with no will but mine. When you find such a one, I will have her.'

150

Having made this forthright statement, the prince leaped on his horse and galloped away to join the hunt which was waiting for him outside the city.

He rode quickly over the fields and meadows until he came to where his huntsmen were resting on the grass. They all rose eagerly to greet him, and all the creatures of the woodland trembled at the sound of the horn. The dogs strained at the leash until it was all their handlers could do to hold them.

On being told by one of his followers that a scent had been

found and all was ready, the prince gave the signal for the hunt
to begin. The hounds were loosed on the trail of the stag and soon
the whole forest resounded with the clamour of neighing horses
and the deep baying of hounds, while the musical notes of the
horn echoed and re-echoed and finally died away in the deepest
recesses of the woods.

Now chance, or fate, led the prince down a hidden path where
none of his huntsmen followed him. The farther he went the
more lost he became, until at last he wandered so far that the
sound of hound and horn could no longer be heard. But the place
to which this odd little adventure had brought him was so full of
natural beauty, so innocent and lovely, that he blessed his mistake.
The clear streams and tall, shady trees filled his mind with awe.

As he was musing gently, inspired by the trees, the cool grass
and rippling water, he was suddenly struck by the sweetest
and loveliest sight that had ever met his eyes. A young shepherdess
sat spinning beside the stream, deftly twirling her spindle as she
watched her flock. She was lovely enough to soften the fiercest
heart. Her skin was lily-white, its purity protected by the shady
groves among which she lived, her mouth had a childish sweetness
and her eyes, shaded by dark lashes, were bluer than the sky itself
and brighter. Gasping with delight, the prince slipped among the
trees and stared, wonderingly, at her beauty; but the sound of
his movement disturbed the lovely girl. No sooner did she look
up and see him than a deep flush spread over her glorious complexion and her face was crimsoned with modest blushes.

This maidenly modesty revealed to the prince a simplicity

153

and gentleness of which he had believed the fair sex incapable until he saw them in all their beauty.

Overcome by a bashfulness that was quite new to him, he stepped forward, fumbling for words. He was more timid than she, but he managed to tell her in a trembling voice that he had

lost track of all his huntsmen and ask whether the hunt had passed anywhere near these woods.

'No one has come to this lonely place, my lord,' she said, 'except yourself. But you need not fear, I will set you back on a familiar path.'

'I thank heaven for this happy chance,' he said. 'I have known these woods for a long time, but never until today did I discover the most precious thing they hold.'

Seeing the prince kneel down on the muddy river bank to

quench his thirst in the flowing brook, the shepherdess exclaimed: 'Wait, my lord!' Then she hurried into her cottage to fetch a cup and handed it, with a sweet smile, to the dazzled prince.

Never had any crystal or agate goblet, glittering with gold and fashioned with the most exquisite skill, seemed to the prince half as beautiful as the little earthenware bowl the shepherdess had given him.

Then they set out together through the woods, up steep rocks and over rushing torrents to find the prince an easy way back to the city.

At every turn the prince was careful to make a mental note of his surroundings. He was so much in love that he was already thinking of returning. At last the shepherdess led him to a cool, dark glade from which the gilded roofs of his splendid palace away across the plain could be seen glittering through the branches.

The prince was very sad at parting from the lovely girl and as he walked slowly away the memory of her face was still imprinted on his heart. The thought of his delightful adventure beguiled his journey home, but the next day he was so badly in love that he felt utterly wretched and miserable, and did not know what to do with himself.

He went hunting again as soon as he could and cleverly escaped from his followers to wander away blissfully among the trees and steep rocks he had taken such care to remember. Guided by his faithful love he avoided all the false trails which crossed his path and found his way to his shepherdess's cottage.

He had found out that her name was Griselda and that she lived

all alone with her father. They led a quiet life, drinking the milk from their flock, making their own clothes from the fleece which the girl herself spun, and needing nothing from the city.

The more he saw of her, the more he loved her and she seemed to him to possess every virtue. He was so happy in his first love that he summoned his council without delay and addressed them as follows:

'As you wished me to, I have finally decided to get married. The bride I am taking is not from a foreign land. She is lovely, good and gently born, and I have chosen her from among our

own people, just as my fathers have done before me. But I shall wait for the wedding day itself before telling you of my choice.'

The news spread like wildfire and it would be impossible to describe the joy and enthusiasm with which the people heard it. Happiest of all was the famous orator, who believed that it was all due to him. 'Nothing,' he told himself proudly, 'can withstand real eloquence.'

How funny it was to see all the pretty girls in the city wasting their time trying to attract the prince's choice. He had said time and again that only a chaste and modest bearing could please him, and so now they were all changing their ways and their dress. They grew pious and soft-spoken, cut down the height of their headdresses by a good six inches, and wore high necks and long sleeves with only the very tips of their fingers peeping out.

The whole city was busy preparing for the wedding. As the days went by every craftsman seemed to be at work. There were splendid coaches made in wonderful new shapes and glittering all over with gold. Stands were erected so that people would be able to get a good view of the procession, and there were vast triumphal arches celebrating love's victory over the great warrior prince.

Arrangements were made for tremendous displays of fireworks, a fantastic ballet and an opera with a cast of thousands, the most beautiful ever to come out of Italy. Rehearsals of the lovely melodies could be heard all day long.

At last the great day arrived. The clear, pale sky was scarcely touched by the pink and gold and silver of the dawn before

159

every girl was up and out of bed. Crowds were collecting everywhere, and guards were posted in strategic positions to hold back the people. The royal palace rang with bugle calls, and with the sound of flutes, oboes and more homely instruments, while the drums and trumpets could be heard all over the city.

At last the prince appeared, surrounded by his court. A great cry of joy went up from the people, but what was their surprise when they saw him take the road leading to the near-by forest, just as usual. 'There,' they said, 'he has always cared more for hunting than for anything else, and now he even prefers it to love.'

To the astonishment of his followers, the prince galloped swiftly across the open parkland towards the mountains and then on into the depths of the forest. Winding his way along countless paths which love had made familiar, he came at last to the humble cottage where his sweetheart lived.

Griselda had heard about the wedding and was at that very moment stepping out of the house, dressed in her best clothes, ready to go and see the procession.

'Where are you running off to?' the prince asked, gazing at her fondly. 'Do not hurry, gentle shepherdess. The wedding you are going to, and where I am to be the bridegroom, will not take place without you. Yes, I love you, and I have chosen you from among a thousand beautiful girls, to spend the rest of my life with. If you will have me, that is.'

'Oh, my lord,' she said, 'I dare not believe that I am destined for such heights of glory. Surely you are making sport of me.'

160

'No, no,' said the prince. 'I mean what I say. Your father knows all about it. (The prince had taken good care to tell him.) Now all you have to do, sweet shepherdess, is graciously consent to be my bride. But if we are to live happily ever after, you must promise me that you will never have any other will but mine.'

'I promise,' she said, 'and I give you my word that were I

to be married to the humblest man in the village I would think it my pleasure to obey him. How much more, then, when you are my lord and master.'

Then the prince presented his bride and, while the whole court cheered, handed her over to the ladies who were to deck her in all the jewels fit for a prince's bride.

The ladies hurried her into the cottage and used all their skill and judgment to make her look as beautiful as possible. They all thought the tiny cottage in the cool shade of a giant plane tree

was a wonderful place to live in and admired the neatness and cleanliness which hid its poverty.

At last the lovely shepherdess came out of the house, all dressed in shining splendour, and everyone marvelled at her beauty, and her magnificent dress. But the prince already felt a pang of regret for the innocent shepherdess.

The shepherdess took her seat in the royal coach of gold and ivory and the prince mounted proudly beside her, feeling just as triumphant as a lover as he ever did riding in a victory procession.

Then, with the whole court following in order of rank and precedence, they set off towards the city. Nearly all the people had poured out into the fields and countryside when they heard of the prince's choice and were waiting impatiently for his return. As he came in sight, they swarmed out to meet him, and the carriage was hardly able to move for the press of people. The joyous shouts of the crowd made the horses shy and tremble so much that they went backwards as often as forwards.

At last they came to the church and, with solemn vows, the

two lovers were made man and wife. Afterwards they went to the palace where a splendid entertainment awaited them, with all kinds of dancing and sports and jousting. The city had never known such a happy day.

In the morning representatives of all the estates of the land came to offer their congratulations to the prince and princess. Surrounded by her ladies, Griselda listened to them with regal composure and answered like a true princess. Everything she did was so graceful and charming that she seemed endowed with every grace of mind and body. She very quickly learned the ways of the great world and from the very first day had picked up all the manners of the court ladies, so that she had no more difficulty in leading them than she had had in leading her sheep.

Before the year was out the happy couple were blessed with a child. It was not the prince they could have wished for, but a little princess so sweet that no one could help loving her. Her father was always coming to look at her and thinking how pretty she was, while as for her mother, she was so delighted that she never took her eyes off the baby.

Griselda was determined to nurse the child herself. 'How could I fail her,' she said, 'when she cries for me? How could I bear to be only half a mother to the child I love?'

Now it may be that the prince was not quite as much in love as he had been when he was first married, or that his bad moods had returned to spread a cloud over his mind and harden his heart, but he began to imagine that the princess was not as good as she seemed. He was hurt by her extraordinary virtue, and

165

thought it was only a trap to deceive him. His mind was so confused that he believed every suspicious rumour that he heard and actually seemed to enjoy doubting his own happiness.

To cure himself of his gloomy suspicions, he took to following her and watching her, and delighted in making her unhappy with tiresome restrictions, frightening her and doing all he could to distinguish truth from falsehood. 'I must not let myself be lulled asleep,' he said. 'If her virtues are real, even the most insufferable treatment will only strengthen them.'

He kept her shut up in the palace, away from all the pleasures of the court. She had to live alone in her room which he would hardly even allow the daylight to enter. Believing that a woman's greatest delight were her jewels and fine clothes, he rudely told her to give back all the pearls and rubies, rings and jewels he had given her as tokens of his love when they were married. She, whose life had always been blameless and whose only thought had been to do her duty, gave them to him willingly and, seeing him pleased to take them back, actually felt as glad to give them as she had been to receive.

'My husband only torments me in order to test me,' she said. 'I can see that he is only making me suffer to stiffen my flagging virtue which might have grown weak with too much rest. And even if that is not his intention, I am sure at least that it is God's will for me. All these troubles are simply a test of my faith and constancy. So many poor women are left to follow their own devices and God lets them wander to the very edge of the abyss without a care for their danger, but out of His simple goodness

166

He has chosen me, and takes trouble to correct me, His beloved child. So I must be grateful for His strictness and be happy in my suffering. I must love this fatherly care, and the hand which is its instrument.'

But even when the prince saw how gladly she obeyed him, he was still not satisfied.

'I see what is at the root of this show of virtue,' he said. 'My blows are useless because they only strike at places where her love no longer is. She lavishes all her affection on her child. If I really want to try her, that is where I should act. Then I shall really find out the truth.'

Griselda was nursing her baby and laughing as she played with it, when he said to her: 'I can see you love her dearly, and yet I must take her away from you, young as she is. It is for her own good, so that she shall be brought up properly and kept safe from the bad habits she will certainly contract if she stays with you. Fortunately, I have found an excellent lady who will bring her up with all the manners and virtues of a real princess. They are coming to fetch her, so prepare to let her go.'

With these words he left her, since even he could not bear to watch the pledge of their love snatched from her arms. Tears streamed down Griselda's face as she waited, in piteous distress, for the moment when she must say goodbye to her baby.

When they came to carry out the cruel deed she only said: 'I must obey.' Then she took the child and gazed at it, kissed it lovingly as it held out its little arms to her and then, weeping, she gave it to them. To the loving mother her grief could not have been more painful had they taken the heart and not the baby from her breast.

Close by the city there was a convent of great antiquity where the holy nuns lived under the austere rule of a pious abbess. Here the child was placed, with no word of who she really was and only a few precious rings as a reward for the care of her.

The prince tried to forget his guilt at this dreadful cruelty by spending his time hunting. He was afraid to face the princess, as a man might be afraid to face a tigress whose cub has been taken from her, and yet she was as kind and gentle to him as ever.

Shame and guilt at such instant obedience only made the prince brood on his imagined wrongs and so, after two days, he wounded

Griselda more deeply still by going to her and telling her their lovely child was dead. And yet, even in her misery at this dreadful, unexpected blow, she seemed to forget her own unhappiness when she looked at her husband's pale face, and to think of nothing but how to comfort him in his pretended grief.

This unparalleled example of her love and affection suddenly softened the prince's cruel heart, so that he very nearly told her their child was still alive. But then his pride and ill nature prevented him and made him think it might be wiser to keep silent.

From that day on the prince and his wife lived together in the utmost love and tenderness and were more fond of one another than ever.

Fifteen years went by with no rift between them, except for an occasional fancy on his part to tease her, but even that was only enough to prevent their love from waning, as a smith will drop water on his fire to keep up the heat.

Meanwhile the young princess was growing in wit and wisdom and turning into the same gentle, innocent creature that her mother was, with just a touch of her noble father's imperious pride. All things combined to make her a perfect beauty.

She shone like a star in every company and it so happened that a young lord of the court saw her at the convent gate and fell violently in love with her.

By the instinct which women, especially beautiful ones, have of knowing the invisible wounds their eyes make as soon as it is done, the princess knew he was in love with her and, with just so much hesitation as was proper, she loved him just as tenderly in return.

The young lover was everything he should be. He was brave, handsome and nobly born, and the prince had long been thinking of making him his son-in-law, so he was delighted to learn that the young people loved one another. But he had a strange fancy to make them earn the greatest happiness of their lives with cruel torments.

'I want to see them happy,' he said, 'but first their love must be tried by uncertainty. And I shall test my wife's patience at the same

time, not to satisfy my own foolish doubts as before (for I can no longer doubt her love), but so that all the world may see how good and gentle and truly wise she is and thank heaven for it with proper reverence.'

He announced publicly that since he was without an heir to rule his people after him, and since the only daughter born of his love match had died in infancy, he must look for better fortune elsewhere. The lady he meant to marry was of illustrious birth and had until this time been brought up in complete innocence in a convent.

The effect of this dreadful news on the young lovers can easily be imagined. Next the prince informed his own faithful wife, with no sign of grief or regret, that they must part or worse would follow, because the people were ashamed of her humble birth and insisted on his taking a noble princess to wife.

'You must go back to your cottage,' he told her, 'and put on your shepherdess's clothes again. I have had them all put ready for you.'

The princess heard her fate with her usual quiet constancy, but beneath her calm appearance she was bitterly hurt. Great tears fell from her lovely eyes, without in the least diminishing her beauty, which shone like sunshine through the rain in spring.

'You are my husband,' she sighed, on the point of fainting, 'my lord and master, and however terrible it may be, I would have you know that my dearest wish is to obey you.'

She withdrew at once alone into her chamber and without a word she took off her fine clothes and put on the dress she had worn to guard her sheep, though her heart was heavy as she did so.

In this simple attire she went to the prince and said to him: 'I cannot leave you without begging your forgiveness for anything

I may have done to displease you. I can bear the weight of my own grief, but not of your anger, my lord. Grant my sad heart this one boon and I shall live content in my poor house and time shall never change my humble, faithful love for you.'

Her gentle, submissive manner and the ragged clothes she wore both at the same moment awakened all the love the prince had felt for her at first sight and almost wrecked his doom of banishment. She was so charming that he was on the point of stepping forward with tears in his eyes to take her in his arms, when pride in surmounting his feelings and gaining a victory over his love suddenly made him answer sternly:

'I have forgotten all the past. I accept your repentance. Go now, it is time to part.'

Griselda turned away and, finding her father dressed once again in his country clothes, bewildered by this sudden change of fortune, she said to him: 'Let us go back to our dark forest and live in our lonely glades again. We can leave the grandeur of palaces without regret. Our cottage is not so splendid, but there at least we may live a simple life in peace and quiet.'

When, after many trials, she made her way back to her distant home, she took up her distaff once again and sat spinning by the banks of the very stream where the prince had first set eyes on her. She felt no bitterness, and with a quiet heart she prayed heaven a hundred times a day to bless and keep her husband in wealth and honour and grant him his heart's desire. A love which had been fed on kindness could not have been warmer than hers.

176

Meanwhile the dear husband for whom she mourned decided to try her still further. He sent for her to come to him.

When she appeared he said to her: 'Griselda, the princess I am to marry must feel no anxiety about you and me, and so I want you to do all you can to help me make my new love happy. You know how I like things to be done. I want nothing spared to show the world that I am a great prince, deeply in love.

'Use all your skill to prepare her chamber, and let everything be rich and sumptuous, clean and elegant. And to help you to remember always that this is a young princess whom I love most dearly I am going to let you see the person I command you to serve so well.'

With that the princess appeared, more radiantly beautiful than the morning sun as it rises in the east. Griselda's heart lifted with motherly love at the sight of her, and she remembered the happy days gone by. 'Alas,' she thought, 'if my prayers had been granted, my own daughter would now have been nearly as tall and perhaps as lovely.'

Without knowing that she was guided by instinct, she immediate-

ly felt such fondness for the young princess that as soon as the girl had left the room she said to the prince: 'My lord, will you permit me to remind you that this charming young princess, who has been bred to the purple and brought up in elegance and comfort, will never live through the kind of treatment I have

received from you. Poverty and humble birth made me used to work and able to bear all kinds of troubles uncomplainingly, but as she has never known pain or the slightest severity, the first unkind word will be the death of her. Alas, my lord, I beg you to be kind to her.'

'You attend to serving me as best you can,' the prince said harshly. 'A simple shepherdess must not presume to teach me my duty.'

At these words Griselda withdrew in silence, with downcast eyes.

Meanwhile great lords who had been invited to the wedding were arriving from all directions. The prince called them all together in a magnificent hall and before the ceremony began he addressed them as follows:

'Except for hope, there is nothing in this world more deceitful than appearances. I am going to show you a striking example of this. Who would not believe that this young lady, about to marry and become a princess, must be happy and content? And yet she is nothing of the kind. Who could help thinking that this gallant young lord must be glad of the wedding, when he is certain to win the prize over all comers in the tourney? Yet that is not so either.

'Moreover, anyone would surely expect to see Griselda in tears of anger and despair, and yet she makes no complaint and accepts everything with endless patience.

'Lastly, anyone would surely imagine that nothing could equal my own happiness when I see my charming bride-to-be:

180

and yet this marriage would make me the most wretched and unhappy prince in all the world.

'If this seems to you a hard riddle to solve, then a few words will be enough to make all clear. And the same words will dissolve all the sadness you have heard of. For I must tell you that the delightful young person you believe has won my heart is in fact my daughter, and I give her hand to this young lord who loves her deeply and is loved in return.

181

'Know, too, that, deeply moved by the loyalty and patience of the wise and faithful wife I so unworthily drove from my side, I am taking her back to try and make amends for the barbarous treatment she has received from my jealous hands, with all the love I have to offer.

'In future I shall devote myself to forestalling her slightest whim, with more eagerness than I ever did to hurting her in the days of my distrust. And if the tale of her steadfast heart shall

live throughout the ages, I want the glory with which I crown her matchless virtue to be still more famous.'

Suddenly, like a rent in the dark clouds heralding a storm when the sun breaks through and floods the countryside with light and

laughter, the gloom and misery disappeared and everyone was all smiles.

In her delight at hearing she was the prince's daughter, the young princess fell at his feet and embraced him. The prince raised her tenderly and took her to her mother, who was almost fainting from the shock. The steadfast heart which had borne so much grief was overcome by the touch of gladness, and she could only clasp her darling child in her arms and weep.

'Enough,' said the prince. 'There will be time later to indulge your feelings. Now go and dress yourself as befits your rank, for we have a wedding to attend.'

The young lovers were escorted to the church and there they promised to love and cherish one another ever after.

Then all was gaiety. There were splendid tournaments, sports, dancing, music and delicious banquets. All eyes followed Griselda wherever she went and she was praised to the skies for her constancy. The people were so happy and so grateful to their capricious prince that they even congratulated him on his cruel testing of her, because it had given them this proof of a virtue so rare and wonderful, and so becoming to a woman.

The ridiculous wishes

Once there was a poor woodcutter who was very tired of the hard life he had to lead. He was so unhappy that he used to say he was longing to find peace in the next world because all the time he had been in this one an unkind fate had never granted so much as one of his wishes.

One day he was out in the woods, grumbling as usual, when Jupiter appeared before him, thunderbolt in hand. The poor man's terror would be hard to describe.

'I don't want anything, my lord,' he said, flinging himself face down on the ground. 'No wishes, no thunderbolt – is that a bargain?'

'You need not be afraid,' said Jupiter. 'I was moved to hear your complaints and I have come to show you that you have misjudged me. Now, listen. I am the sovereign ruler of all the world and I promise to grant your first three wishes, whatever they may be. That ought to make you happy and content. Only remember, your whole happiness depends on them, so think carefully before you make them.'

With these words Jupiter disappeared again into the sky.

The woodcutter picked up his bundle of faggots and trudged happily home. Never had the weight on his shoulders seemed so light.

'I must be sure not to do anything hasty,' he told himself as he hurried along. 'First of all I must consult my wife.'

'Fanny,' he called out as he went into his cottage, 'let's make up a good fire. We are rich for life. All we have to do is wish.' And thereupon he told her what had happened.

When his wife heard the tale her imagination instantly set to work making tremendous plans but, realizing the importance of acting sensibly in the matter, she said to her husband: 'Blaise, my dear, we must not spoil things by being impatient. We must talk over what we should do. Let us sleep on it and not make our first wish until tomorrow.'

'I quite agree,' the good man said. 'But you go and draw some wine to celebrate.'

When she came back, the woodcutter stretched out comfortably in front of the fire, drinking his wine.

'We've such a good blaze,' he said, leaning back in his chair, 'a length of sausage would go down very nicely. I wish we had some.'

No sooner had he said the words than his wife saw to her astonishment a great length of sausage emerge from the chimney corner and wriggle towards her. She let out a scream, and then realized that it was all due to her silly husband's thoughtless wish. This made her very cross and she began to scold the poor man furiously and call him all kinds of names.

'When we might have had a kingdom,' she said, 'and gold and pearls and rubies and diamonds, and fine clothes – and you have to go and wish for a sausage!'

'I'm sorry,' said her husband, 'I made a mistake. It was a dreadful thing to do, but I will do better next time.'

'Very well,' said his wife, 'but I'll say it till the cows come home: you must be a proper donkey to make such a wish!'

This made the husband so angry that he had half a mind to wish himself a widower (and between ourselves he might have been better off if he had). 'Men are born to misery!' he said. 'I wish the silly sausage was hanging from the end of your nose, you stupid thing!'

Instantly, his wish came true. As he spoke, the sausage fastened itself on his angry wife's nose.

Fanny was furious. She was very pretty, and the plain truth is that the ornament far from improved her looks, quite apart from the fact that it hung down over her face and interfered with her talking. For one glorious moment the advantages of this made her husband think he had nothing left to wish for!

'Now,' he said to himself, 'with the wish I have left, I could make myself a king. There's nothing quite like royalty, after all. But then there is the queen to be thought of. It would be very unkind to make her sit on a throne with a nose a yard long. It is only right that she decide whether she wants to be a queen with that hideous nose, or a woodcutter's wife with her own nose, just like anyone else.'

His wife thought about it and, although she knew that no

192

one would dare criticize her nose once she had a crown, she could not bear not to be admired, and preferred to stay as she was rather than be an ugly queen.

And so the woodcutter did not become a great king with a purse full of gold. He was only too happy to use his last wish simply to put his wife's face right again.

Donkeyskin

Once upon a time there lived a great king. His people loved him, his neighbours and allies respected him and he might have been called the happiest monarch on earth. His choice of a wife set the seal on his happiness, for he married a princess as good as she was lovely and the couple lived together in perfect harmony. They had only one child, a daughter so sweet and charming that they never regretted not having a larger family.

The king had a palace of the utmost splendour and magnificence, his ministers were wise and capable, his courtiers loyal and true-hearted and his servants faithful and hard-working. He had vast stables full of the finest horses imaginable, all gorgeously caparisoned. People came from far and wide to marvel at them, but the thing that always surprised them most of all was an old donkey who stood pricking his ears in the best stall.

Now the king had given the donkey pride of place for a good reason. He was really a most extraordinary animal and deserved the distinction, because every morning the straw in his stable, far from being dirty, was covered with gold coins of all kinds which were collected when he woke up.

At length, since kings, like their subjects, are only mortal, and some bad luck is always mixed with the good, it happened that the queen fell ill of a cruel disease for which not all the skill and cunning of the doctors could find a remedy. There was great grief throughout the land.

When the queen felt her last hour approaching, she said to her weeping husband: 'There is one thing I must ask of you before I die. If you ever wish to marry again —'

At these words the king sobbed pitifully and, taking his wife's hands and bathing them with tears, he swore it was needless to talk to him of a second marriage.

'No, no, my dearest queen,' he said at last, 'speak to me rather of following you!'

But the queen continued, with a firmness which redoubled the king's anguish: 'Your country has a right to expect an heir. I have given you only a daughter and you will be urged to have sons to take after their father. I only beg you, by all the love you have had for me, not to yield to your people's demands until you have found a princess who is better and more beautiful than I. When I have your word for this, I shall die content.'

It may well be that the queen, who did not underestimate herself, had exacted this promise in the belief that she had no equal in the world and so the king would be bound never to marry again.

She died at last and no husband ever mourned more sincerely. The king did nothing but weep and wail, day and night, and put the whole court into the deepest mourning.

But even great griefs do not last for ever, and besides, all the great lords of the land came in a body to ask the king to take another wife.

At first the proposal seemed a cruel one and made him weep afresh. He pleaded his promise to the late queen and challenged his counsellors to find a princess who was better and more beautiful than she, for he was convinced that this was impossible.

However, he promised to think the matter over. In fact he did begin looking round for a marriageable princess to suit him, but there was not one whose portrait was as charming as his late queen, and so he came to no decision.

Then an unfortunate thing happened. The king, who had always been a most sane and sensible man, suddenly went quite mad. He took it into his head that his daughter the princess was incomparably more lovely and intelligent than the queen her mother, and announced that he was determined to marry her, since she alone could absolve him from his vow.

The princess was dreadfully upset, and the only thing she could think of was to go and see her godmother, the Lilac Fairy. She set out that very night in a pretty carriage drawn by a large sheep who knew the way and arrived safely.

The fairy, who was very fond of the princess, told her she knew already all what she had come to tell her, but that she was not to worry, all would be well provided she did exactly as the fairy told her.

'For it would be quite wrong of you to marry your father, my dear,' she said, 'but you may avoid it without defying him.

Tell him he must first give you a dress the colour of the sky. With all his power he will never be able to do that.'

The princess thanked her godmother, and the next morning she did as the fairy advised and told her father the king she would promise nothing unless she had a dress the colour of the sky.

Delighted that she had given him some hope, the king called together all the most celebrated dressmakers and ordered them to make the dress – with the threat that he would hang every one of them if they failed. But he was not obliged to go to such lengths. Two days later they brought him the fabulous dress. Bluer than the bluest of blue skies, girdled with little gilded clouds was this heavenly dress when it was spread before him.

The princess was very bothered and did not know what to do. The king was growing impatient. She went back to her godmother, who was most surprised to hear that her trick had failed. This time she told her to ask for a dress the colour of the moon.

The king could refuse her nothing. He sent for the cleverest dressmakers and ordered them to make a dress the colour of the moon and deliver it within twenty-four hours. The princess was more delighted with the wonderful dress than she was with her father's zeal in obtaining it, and as soon as she was alone with her nurse and her ladies she burst into tears.

The Lilac Fairy, who knew everything that had happened, came to the poor princess's rescue.

'I may be wrong,' she said, 'but I think if you ask for a dress the colour of the sun we shall manage to outwit the king your

205

father. Surely no one will ever be able to make such a dress, and even if they do we shall at least have gained time.'

The princess agreed and asked for the dress, and the lovesick king willingly gave all the diamonds and rubies in his crown to help in the splendid work. He gave orders that no expense must be spared to make the dress rival the sun. When it was displayed all those who saw it had to shut their eyes, so dazzling was the sight. As a matter of fact this was the reason dark glasses were invented.

The princess's feelings can be imagined. A more miraculous piece of work had never been seen. Making the excuse that her eyes were dazzled, the princess retired to her room, utterly overcome. There she found the fairy, more shamed than words can say and, worse still, scarlet with anger at the sight of the dress the colour of the sun.

'This time, my girl,' she told the princess, 'we are going to put your father to a terrible test. I know how set on this marriage he is, but I think your next request will shake him a little. Ask for the skin of the donkey he dotes on so much and which fills his coffers so lavishly. Run along now, and be sure to tell him you want that skin.'

Thinking that her father would never bring himself to sacrifice his donkey, the princess went away, delighted at finding another way of avoiding the hated marriage, and asked her father for the animal's skin.

Astonished though the king was at this whim, he did not hesitate to gratify it. The poor donkey was slain and its skin presented to the princess. Seeing no other way of escape, she was almost in despair when her godmother came to her.

'What are you about, my child?' she said when she saw the princess tearing her hair and scratching her lovely cheeks. 'This is the happiest moment of your life. Wrap yourself in this skin, leave the palace and go wherever the road may carry you. When a person gives up everything for the sake of what is right, the gods will certainly reward them. Off you go, and I will see to it that your belongings follow wherever you go. At each place where you stop you will find that a chest containing your clothes and jewels follows you under the ground. Moreover, I will give you my magic wand. Tap the ground with it when you have need of your chest and it will appear before your eyes. But be off, quickly, and waste no time.'

The princess kissed her godmother again and again, begging her not to desert her. Then she dirtied her face with soot from the fire, covered herself with the ugly skin and left the grand palace, without being recognized by anyone.

The princess's disappearance caused a great to-do. The king was in despair. He had made all the preparations for a splendid feast and nothing would console him. He sent over a hundred militiamen and over a thousand musketeers out in search of his daughter, but the guardian fairy made her invisible to the most skilful searchers, and so there was nothing he could do about it.

Meanwhile, the princess trudged on, farther and farther away, and then farther still. Everywhere she looked for work, but although people gave her food out of charity they always thought she was so dirty that no one wanted her.

At last, however, she came to a fine city, and just outside

208

the gates was a small farm where the woman needed a girl to do the rough work and clean out the geese and pigs. Seeing the grubby traveller, she offered her the place and the princess was so tired and had walked so far that she accepted gratefully.

She was given a corner of the scullery to sleep in and for the first few days she was a laughing stock for the rest of the servants because she was so foul and disgusting in her donkey skin. But at last they grew used to her, and besides, she was so careful about her work that the farmer's wife took her under her wing.

She minded the sheep and put them in the fold in bad weather, she took the geese out to pasture, and learned as fast as if she had been born to it. Everything she turned her hand to she did well.

She was sitting one day beside a clear pool, feeling very sorry

for herself, when she caught sight of her reflection. The hideous donkeyskin which covered her from head to foot filled her with horror. Dreadfully ashamed of her appearance, she washed her face and hands until her skin was whiter than ivory and her cheeks fresh and glowing again. The joy of finding herself beautiful again made her want to bathe, although afterwards she had to put on her shameful skin once more to return to the farm.

Luckily the next day was a holiday and she was free to open her chest and dress up in her beautiful clothes. She powdered her silken hair and put on her dress the colour of the sky. Her room was so small there was not room to spread out the train of the wonderful dress. The lovely princess gazed wonderingly at her reflection in her mirror, as well she might, and resolved to amuse herself on Sundays and holidays by dressing up in all her dazzling dresses in turn, and this she did most faithfully.

She would twine flowers and diamonds skilfully into her glorious hair and often sighed to think that there was no one to see her beauty but her sheep and geese, who loved her just as much in her horrible donkeyskin, which was now the name she was known by at the farm.

One holiday, when Donkeyskin was wearing her dress the colour of the sun, the king's son, to whom the farm belonged, happened to stop there to rest on his way home from hunting.

The prince was young and very handsome, dearly loved by his father and mother and the darling of his people. When he had finished the simple supper they had offered him he began roaming about, poking into all the odd corners of the farm.

As he wandered round, he found himself in a dark passage at the end of which he could see a closed door. Curiosity impelled him to put his eye to the keyhole. Imagine his surprise when he saw a princess so beautiful and so magnificently dressed that from her sweet, proud air he thought she must be a goddess at least. But for the respect the entrancing vision inspired, he would have burst the door down then and there.

Reluctantly he turned his back on the dark passageway, but he was still determined to find out who lived in that small room. The people told him it was a servant girl known as Donkeyskin because of the filthy old skin she wore as a cloak, and added that she was so filthy and slatternly no one could bear to look at her or speak to her, and they had only taken her in out of pity, to attend to the sheep and geese.

The prince was by no means satisfied with this explanation, but he could see that the ignorant peasants knew no more and it was useless to question them. He went back to his father's palace head over heels in love and unable to get out of his mind the divinely beautiful vision he had glimpsed through the key-

hole. He was sorry now that he had not knocked on the door, and made up his mind to do so next time without fail.

But his passionate love heated his blood to such a ferment that by that very same night he was in a raging fever, and even his life was in danger. His mother, the queen, was in despair when no remedy would do him any good, because he was her only child. She promised the doctors enormous rewards, but all in vain. Not all their cunning could cure the prince.

At last they diagnosed the cause of his decline as a fatal grief, and told the queen, who went at once to her son and asked him tenderly to tell her the reason for his unhappiness. If it were the crown he desired, she said, his father the king would gladly abdicate in his favour, or if there were some princess he loved they would make any concessions to obtain her for him, even should the king be at war with her country and no matter how just his cause. Only she implored him not to die, because their own lives depended on his.

Before the unhappy queen had come to the end of this piteous speech, the prince's face was wet with tears.

'Mother,' he said to her at last, in a weak voice, 'I am not such a bad son as to covet my father's crown. He will live for many years yet, I trust, and I shall always be his most loyal and obedient subject! As for the princesses you offer me, I have not thought of marrying yet, but you may be sure that I am ruled by your wishes and will always obey you, whatever the cost.'

'Oh, my son,' said the queen, 'no price would be too high to save your life. But, my dearest son, save mine and your royal father's by telling us what it is you desire, and rest assured you shall have it.'

'Very well, Mother,' said the prince, 'since you will have me tell you what is in my mind, I will obey you. It would be wicked of me to endanger the lives of two people so dear to me. Yes, Mother, I want Donkeyskin to bake me a cake and have it brought to me when it is made.'

The queen was perplexed by the strange name and she asked who Donkeyskin might be.

One of her guard, who happened to have seen the girl, told her: 'It is the ugliest of all creatures after the wolf, Your Majesty, a dirty slut of a girl who lives at your farm and keeps your geese.

'Never mind,' said the queen. 'Perhaps my son tasted her

cooking on his way home from hunting and he has taken this fancy because he is ill. At all events I will have Donkeyskin (since there is such a creature) bake him a cake at once.'

Messengers hurried to the farm to fetch Donkeyskin and command her to make the best cake she could for the prince.

There are some who say that when the prince put his eye to the keyhole, Donkeyskin had caught sight of him, and that afterwards she had looked out of her little window and seen the handsome young prince, and remembered him often with many a sigh.

Be that as it may, whether Donkeyskin had actually seen him or had heard everyone singing his praises, she was delighted at the chance to make herself known to him. She shut herself up in her tiny room, threw off her horrible skin, washed her face and hands and bound up her lovely hair. Then she dressed herself in a bodice of shining silver with a skirt to match, and using the whitest flour and the freshest butter and eggs, she began to make the longed-for cake.

It may have been an accident, or then again it may not, but as she worked a ring slipped off her finger and fell into the mixture. When the cake was ready she put on her nasty skin and gave the cake to the guard. She asked for news of the prince, but the man hurried off to carry the cake to his master without bothering to reply.

The prince took the cake eagerly and ate it so hungrily that his doctors shook their heads and called it a bad sign. In point of fact the prince very nearly choked on the ring, which he found in a mouthful of cake, but he took it out of his mouth and stopped gobbling cake while he examined the brilliant emerald in a gold setting. The ring was so small, he thought it must fit the prettiest little finger in the world.

He smothered the ring with kisses, popped it under his pillow and took it out whenever he thought no one was looking. He was at his wits' end to think how he might see the girl to whom the ring belonged. He dared not imagine that if he asked for Donkeyskin who had baked the cake for him, he would be allowed to see her, nor could he admit to what he had seen through the keyhole for fear of being scoffed at for a madman. He was so worried that his fever grew worse and the doctors, in despair, told the queen he

217

was sick of love. The king and queen hurried grieving to their son's bedside.

'My dear, dear son,' cried the unhappy monarch, 'tell us the name of the girl you love and we promise that you shall have her, were she the lowest slave!'

The queen kissed him and added her word to the king's. The prince was deeply moved.

'Mother and Father,' he said, 'I do not aim to make a match that would displease you, and to prove it' – he pulled the emerald from under his pillow – 'I will marry the girl who can wear this ring, whoever she may be. A girl with such a pretty finger could scarcely be a coarse peasant.'

The king and the queen took the ring and examined it closely. They came to the same conclusion as the prince, that the ring could only belong to a girl of noble family. The king kissed his son and, telling him to get better quickly, he went outside and ordered the drums and trumpets and fifes to be sounded all through the city, while heralds proclaimed that any maiden who came to the palace might try on the ring. She whom it fitted should marry the heir to the throne.

The princesses came first, and then the duchesses, marchionesses and baronesses, but no matter how they squeezed their fingers it was no use. None of them could wear the ring. Next they had to try the ordinary little girls, but, pretty as they were, their fingers were all too big. The prince was much better by now and made the trial himself. At last they came to the servant-girls, but they were no better, until there was no one who had not tried the ring: kitchenmaids, scullerymaids and shepherdesses had all been brought to the prince, but their stubby red fingers all stuck at the very top.

'Have you brought Donkeyskin, who made me the cake?' said the prince.

Everyone laughed and told him 'no', because she was much too dirty.

'Then fetch her at once,' said the king. 'It shall not be said I left anyone out.'

They ran off with shouts of laughter to fetch the goose-girl.

The princess had heard the drums and heralds and guessed that her ring had something to do with the uproar. She loved the prince but, because true love is shy and modest, she had been in constant fear lest some lady should have a finger as small as her own. She was overcome with joy when they came and knocked on her door.

When she heard of the search for a finger to fit the ring, some wild hope had made her dress her hair with special care and put on her lovely silver bodice and the skirt of flounced silver lace studded with emeralds. When she heard the knock on her door and voices calling her to go to the prince, she quickly put on her donkeyskin and opened the door. The jeering messengers told her the king wanted her to go and marry his son and led her to the prince amid shouts of laughter. Even he was a little startled when he saw her and could scarcely believe that this was his proud and lovely vision. Bewildered and disappointed at his

220

dreadful mistake, he said: 'Are you the girl who lives at the end of the dark passage off the farmyard?'

'Yes, Your Highness,' she said.

'Show me your hand,' he told her trembling, and gave a deep sigh.

Then, what was the surprise of the king and queen and all the chamberlains and great lords of the court when, from beneath the filthy black skin, there emerged a little delicate hand, all pink and white, with the prettiest little finger in the world on to which the ring slipped easily. The princess gave her shoulders a little shake, the donkeyskin fell to the ground and she stepped forth, so dazzling in her beauty that the prince, who was still very weak, fell down and clasped her knees with a passion which made her blush. But no one noticed because the king and queen stepped forward and hugged her with all their might and asked her if she would indeed marry their son.

Overcome by the love and affection showered on her by the handsome young prince, the princess was on the point of thanking

them when the ceiling opened and the Lilac Fairy appeared in a chariot made of branches and flowers of her own tree. With great eloquence she told the princess's story and the king and queen, in their delight at learning that Donkeyskin was a real princess, kissed her more lovingly than ever. The prince, however, was still more moved by the princess's constancy and loved her the more for the knowledge.

He could hardly wait to marry the princess and would barely allow time to prepare for such a magnificent wedding. The king and queen doted on their daughter-in-law and made a great fuss of her. She had insisted that she could not marry the prince without permission from her father the king, and he was the first to receive an invitation, although he was not told the name of the bride. The Lilac Fairy, who was naturally in charge of the arrangements, had suggested this as a sensible precaution.

Kings came from every land, some borne in litters, others in carriages. The furthest came riding on elephants, tigers or eagles. But the greatest and most powerful of all was the princess's father. Fortunately he had forgotten all about his foolish infatuation and had married a very lovely widowed queen, but had no more children. When the princess ran to meet him he knew her at once and kissed her tenderly before she had time to throw herself at his feet, and when the king and queen presented their son he was kindness itself to the prince. The wedding took place with all possible splendour, although the young couple cared little for the pomp and had eyes only for each other.

On the same day, the king had his son crowned king, and,

223

kissing his hand, placed him on his own throne. Despite his protests his loving son was forced to obey. The wedding festivities continued for nearly three months, and the love of the bride and bridegroom was so great that it would be lasting still, if they had not both died about a hundred years afterwards.